PATRICK GLOUTNEY

MIRAGE

STONECROFT PUBLISHING

Create Space Edition
Copyright © 2020 by Patrick Gloutney

ISBN: 978-0-9947251-9-6

Cover photo © 2012, Jarin13
Cover design © 2020, Patrick Gloutney

To my friend, Elizabeth Peltz, who's whimsical and always positive

nature never ceases to inspire and amaze.

Blind belief in authority is the greatest enemy of truth—Albert Einstein

Mirage

1. West Wind Flight Track, Safety Command

Karly watched in horror as her brother, Nate, sped around the airborne race track. It was fascinating to see the things that Nate could push his aircraft to do, but it was horrifying knowing the dangers involved in Air Racing. Karly would know. She worked as the chief safety coordinator at the race track where the semi-finals were being held. She had seen all too well what happened if a pilot timed a turn wrong, or worse, hit another aircraft.

"And *Starship* takes the lead followed closely behind by *Claw's Breath* and *Firefly*," the announcer's voice boomed over the track's PA system. The racers were entering the final leg of the race. She watched the cameras as the racers sped by. Nate's aircraft, the *Firefly*, had a different design than all the others; rather than fixed wings it had varying wing sweep controls. It gave the aircraft more maneuverability during slow flight but robbed it of maneuverability during high-speed flights and Nate almost never flew slowly. She watched as they took a turn, the three leading aircraft separated by mere inches. The wings of the *Firefly* snapped forward to pull it into the turn putting it in the lead. It re-established itself on the straight away, folding its wings back as it gained speed towards the finish line.

Patrick Gloutney

"Do we have the safeties in place at the finish line?" Karly asked.

"Yes m'am," her second in command reported. The most common crash the track experienced was pilots that were too excited after winning a race forgetting the track takes a turn after the finish line. It was designed for them to bleed off extra airspeed but often times they never reduced power and plowed into the wall. As a result, Karly had designed a type of safety net that would catch the plan before it slammed into the wall.

Her command center was right by the finish line, so rather than watch the final turn of the race on her hologram display she turned to the window.

"*Firefly's* taking the final turn hot, followed closely by *Claw's Breath*," the announcer called. Then out of nowhere *Starship* came careening between the two aircraft. It rolled into a knife edge and slipped between the wing tips of both *Firefly* and *Claw's Breath*. It then rolled out and made for the final obstacle. It was a small ring that the aircraft had to pass through. If pilots were off by even a foot, then they wouldn't make it. As a result, the racers had limits on their wingspans. It was what inspired the wing sweep design on the *Firefly;* more wing with a shortened span. She watched as *Starship* approached the ring.

"*Starship's* not going to make it," she called. Sure enough, *Starship's* left-wing tip caught the edge of the ring. It tore off, throwing the aircraft into a flat spin.

"Activate shields," Karly ordered. The shields were in place to prevent aircraft from slamming into the spectators. The problem with them was that their radiation output was too high to be left on. Shimmers of silver appeared in front of the spectators and *Starship* hit hard, exploding into a fireball and falling to the deck of the race track. The pilot would not have survived the crash. This all happened in a mere second. Karly expertly turned her attention back to the remaining racers, forgoing emotional response for the time being. She hated losing a racer but she would never forgive herself if she lost others because she was distracted.

The remaining aircraft sped towards the finish line. Nate was losing by about a nose length. Karly prayed that he wouldn't do anything stupid. She feared losing him, he was all she had left after their parents died. She watched, much to her dismay, as the *Firefly* rolled over the top of the *Claw's Breath* forcing it to descend.

Firefly then took the lead. Karly shook her head. That was technically an illegal move. She was about to call him on it when *Claw's Breath* bumped the *Firefly's* horizontal stabilizer. The aircraft bucked and skidded out of control. Karly didn't hesitate. Not only were her actions for Nate's safety but an out of control aircraft like that could cause a lot of damage.

"Safety command to all racers! Break immediately! I say again break, break, break!" She ordered. The remaining racers went into steep climbs away from the race track to get out of danger. Karly watched as her brother fought with his aircraft for control. It skidded around the track and bucked; its pitch controls clearly damaged.

C'mon Nate, she urged. Her hope faded as the *Firefly* reared up on its wing and slammed into the protection shields. A bright flash appeared and the aircraft vanished.

2. City of the Clouds

Armine flexed his wings as he made his way towards the race track. It was going to be a good day, a very good day. Today he would take the championship and hopefully the heart of his infatuation. He smiled as he entered the waiting area for competitors. He tucked his wings tightly against his back so as not to take more room than necessary. He looked around the gathered people and instantly spotted her. Nafais, Princess of the Sky. There was no missing her with her stunning beauty and multi-colored wings. The only being that rivaled her beauty was that of her mother, Queen Rosaria, Queen of the Clouds. Armine was rather familiar with the royal family. He and Nafais had forged a strong friendship over the years. Armine saw a clear spot and spread his wings; he took off like a shot and landed next to the princess.

"Princess Nafais," he addressed. Nafais smiled at him. They had grown up together, playing in the skies. They had been the best of friends and still were. The only problem was that with their duties they were often kept apart. Armine was Captain of the Guard in charge of protecting the City of the Clouds, where they resided, and often spent a long night in his command ensuring all ran smoothly.

"Captain. I trust that you will show us all a good time today?" Nafais responded respectfully. Armine smiled; the Guard Race was the highlight of the year in the city for sure. All the guards that participated would fly at breakneck speeds through the streets of the city in order to see who was the fastest. Every year for the past four years Armine had won and he intended to do so again this year. Only this time he hoped his prize would be more than a medal.

"Rest assured my Princess. It will be a sight to behold. Perhaps afterward you will accompany me to a dinner?" Armine asked, sporting a confident grin.

Nafais's smile faltered slightly before she put it back on, "Perhaps."

Armine felt his heart sink. He had never given rejection much consideration. He and the princess were so close. It seemed logical to him that they would eventually become more. He didn't let his disappointment show though, "Of course. Now I must return to my place, good day Princess." With that, he flew off.

***

Mirage

The race was about to begin; it was only a matter of seconds now. Adrenaline rushed through Armine's veins as he readied himself for the release, making him forget about Nafais' rejection. He had a race to win. Tightening his muscles so his wings would spring downward once he released them, he kept his arms at the ready, not wanting an increased drag on his body. Then the horn sounded. Armine took to the air quickly, accelerating past the other competitors. He took the first sharp turn seconds before a bright flash of light erupted. It dazed him and he went careening into a cloud. When he looked up, he saw the guards in the race had suffered the same fate. A large creature flew overhead. Armine watched it disappear into the city center. Its large wings never beat but a loud constant roar could be heard coming from it. Armine wasted no time. He and his guards were at the armory in a mere moment and then back on the hunt for the creature. It had picked the worst moment to attack them; with most of the guards disarmed for the race, it had time to inflict damage.

The guards split up, searching every street. Armine was the one to find it, only it wasn't the way he had hoped. The creature flew around a corner and surprised him. He ducked for cover as it flew by.

What is this thing? he asked himself, as he gave chase. Whatever it was, it was certainly fast. He was barely keeping up. It was amazing the turns this thing made. Even though Armine was smaller, he had difficulty making the tight corners at these speeds. He raised his bow and arrow and let loose a shot. It merely glanced off the creature body. Two other guards soon joined him.

"It must have armor. Cut it off!" Armine ordered. The guards complied and were soon surrounding the creature. It never even slowed down, plowing through one of the guards in its way.

"Goddess of the Sky," Armine muttered. This thing was ruthless. He sped after it, making multiple attempts to stop it only to fail each time. It was now approaching the castle. He looked ahead in time to see Princess Nafais standing in the creature's path.

"Nafais! It won't stop!" His cries were lost over the roar of the creature. He watched in fear as Nafais simply raised a hand. Armine beat his wings furiously but it was no use, he could never pass the creature. Then suddenly the wind shifted and Armine felt the lift under his wings vanish. He fell to the street. When he looked up the creature had fallen, landing on black rounded feet. There it sat motionless and quiet. Armine ran to the Princess.

Mirage

"Nafais what did you think you were doing?" he asked angrily, dropping the titles since they were alone.

"Relax Armine. I stopped it didn't I?"

"That was incredibly stupid," Armine snapped. Strangled cries began to come from the creature; Nafais pushed past Armine and approached it.

"Shh...it's okay now," she soothed the beast, patting its nose.

"You can't be serious!" Armine protested.

"It is still a being of the sky. I intend to protect it, not harm it, I think," Nafais replied.

"What do you mean 'you think' dear daughter?" the Queen asked from behind them. Armine quickly fell to his knees in front of the Queen. "Rise Captain."

"It's cold. Like it's made of metal," Nafais responded as she moved along its flanks. The Queen remained silent. Then part of the beast opened and something climbed out.

"I believe that is the creature you wish to protect," the Queen said.

"A human. Impossible! They are but legends and they cannot fly..." Armine argued, but the Queen silenced him. He watched as Nafais approached the human. The man appeared scared out of his wits. He tried to run but fell. Nafais picked him up and set him on his feet.

"It is alright," she reassured. "We mean you no harm if you mean us none."

Armine saw a smile creep onto the Queen's face as she watched her daughter. He too watched in fascination as the Princess soothed the being. He looked at the beast he had chased. It must have been enslaved to carry the human, but why?

"Daughter," the Queen called, "bring him here."

Nafais complied and brought the human to her mother. Her mother waved a hand over the human and he fell asleep.

"Mother!" Nafais protested.

"Captain?" the Queen asked.

Armine looked to his Queen, "Yes your majesty?"

Mirage

"See to it that this man's steed is well cared for. You and the Princess shall be charged with determining the reason for his presence when he awakens. Understood?"

"Yes, my Queen," Armine responded, not sure how he was going to care for the creature he had chased through the city streets.

3. City of the Clouds

Nate groaned as he woke up. He rolled over to find himself in a very large bed. He opened his eyes to see that he was in a lavish room. He shot straight up and frantically looked around the room. It definitely wasn't the hospital room he was expecting to wake up in after that last race. The last thing he remembered was hitting the protection shields. He tested all his limbs; he seemed fine. He got to his feet and made it to the window. His mouth fell open at the sight outside. The city before him glittered in the moonlight. Tall towers that looked like they had been made out of clouds extended from the streets below him. It looked like something out a movie, with extravagantly designed pillars of the cloud like material and beautiful architecture. *Is this what heaven looks like?* Then he heard voices.

"I'm telling you Nafais it won't move. I have tried everything! It won't even eat anything, and it's been almost two days!" one rough voice exclaimed.

"Maybe your being too forceful," a much more soothing voice responded, "I will have a look at it once I check on our guest."

Mirage

When the door opened Nate froze. The guy who approached him was huge, at least six and a half feet tall, with well-toned muscles and a face that said: "don't mess with me". What shocked Nate more were the black wings that extended from the man's back. Before he could react another more colorful winged creature entered the room.

"Stand down Armine," that soothing voice instructed, "He is not our enemy."

"He wreaked havoc in our streets," the other protested.

"Yet made no attempt to cause harm," the soothing voice reasoned, "Now go, see to it that his steed is ready for my arrival." With that, the man with black wings left and the multi-colored wing retracted to its owner. "I apologize for Captain Armine. You caused quite the stir with your arrival."

Nate was at a loss for words. Before him stood the most beautiful creature he had ever seen. She stood shorter than the other man, only about six feet tall, with green eyes and long pale blonde, almost white, hair that cascaded down her shoulders. She wore a stunning sky-blue dress decorated with lines of gold colored fabric coursing through it like veins and had a magnificent set of multi-colored wings.

She gave him a warm smile, "Where are my manners, my name is Nafais, Princess of the Sky."

Nate could barely breath but did manage to produce one word, "What?"

Nafais chuckled, "What might your name be?"

"Uhm..."

"Do not be afraid. I mean you no harm, nor do I intend to harm the steed that brought you here," Nafais reassured.

"The what?"

Nafais sighed, "Do you know where you are?"

Nate shook his head, "Last I checked I was dead."

Nafais gave a small dignified laugh. "You are not dead. You are in the City of the Clouds. A place most of the supposedly ground-bound creatures could only dream of seeing. Yet you found something to bring you here."

Mirage

Nate again stared at the woman before him, *She's nuts,* he told himself. Despite his incredulity there was something about her that made him want to believe her. Almost like a whisper in the back of his mind telling him to trust her, unconditionally.

"Nathan," he finally spoke, "My name is Nathan. Most people call me Nate"

Nafais smiled again, "That was not so hard now was it?"

"So uhm..." Nate scratched the back of his neck, "How far are we from the West Wind Flight Track?"

Nafais tilted her head, her smile slipping slightly, "I am afraid I do not know of where you speak."

Nate was going to question how she didn't know the most famous race track in the world but quickly resigned himself to the fact that he was worst then lost. *Karly,* he thought suddenly.

"I have to get back," he said frantically.

"Whatever do you mean?" Nafais asked.

"To the race track. I have to get to Karly!" Nate started towards the door but a wing stopped him.

"Is Karly the name of the steed you rode in on?" Nafais asked.

"No, She's my sister; she's going to be worried sick if I don't get back."

"What happened to you?" Nafais asked, "Your species is but a legend here. Where did you come from?"

Nate tried to get past the wing blocking his path but it proved impossible, "I'm a racer. I fly that...um, that *steed* in competitions to make a living. I was nearing the finish line when some idiotic pilot bumped my tail and sent me skidding out of control. Last thing I remember before waking up here was hitting the safety shields," Nate explained.

"And your sister?" Nafais asked.

"I'm the only family she has left!" Nate yelled.

Nafais retracted her wing, "Let us care for your steed and we will find a way to return you to your sister."

4. West Wind Flight Track

Thunder could be heard below them as Karly stood in the middle of the racetrack covered by a big winter coat. They had moved the race track above the storm so it would remain undamaged but that meant thinner and cooler air. Despite the cold, she stood transfixed on one spot. The last race haunted her. She knew what was coming as soon as she saw *Starship* make that knife edge turn to get first place. The pilot had no time to correct his position relative to the ring. That crash was peculiar enough, the pilot had managed to eject before being killed in the crash. *Starship's* wreckage had fallen to the floor leaving burning fuel on the safety shields. The other racers had flown off as soon as she ordered the end of the race and *Claw's Breath's* pilot was reprehended for his actions in the race. Just as Nate would have been. Karly stared at the spot where Nate had hit the safety shields. It didn't make sense. The shields acted like a wall. They were like hitting a freaking wall. They didn't make a plane vanish. Yet the *Firefly* had disappeared into thin air. No fire, no wreckage, not even a fuel stain as it hit the shields hard enough to cause them to short out. She grimaced as she remembered the burning fuel and debris from *Starship's* crash falling onto the crowd.

Karly sighed; she had failed today. Not only had she lost a racer but she had lost ten spectators and injured countless others as well. She turned and headed inside. Her boss, Damion, would be waiting for her report in her office. She couldn't stall any longer.

She reached the office moments later and sure enough, Damion was waiting.

"Karly, what happened today?" he asked.

"To put it simply, idiots happened. We need to enforce the rules better," Karly responded.

Her boss nodded, "You have no idea. But the high ups say that the audience likes the defiance."

Karly sighed, "I lost eleven lives today to defiance."

"So what happened?"

Karly began to run the footage of the race, "*Starship* made quite the pull ahead, not technically illegal but ill-advised. He didn't have enough time to correct his position. The hit took out his wing, sending him spinning, I raised the shields and he hit. *Firefly* made to cut off *Claw's Breath* who bumped him in retaliation. Then *Firefly* hit the shields and...everything went dark."

Mirage

"Dark?" Damion asked.

"I don't know why but *Firefly's* hit shorted out the entire safety system. My command lost all power. As a result...well, you saw the bodies."

Karly's boss grunted his acknowledgment, "Have they recovered the wreckage?" Karly simply shook her head, "Are you alright? I am no fool. I know the *Firefly* was flown by your brother. I'm also not so insensitive that I don't understand the impact that can have on someone."

"I'm fine. I just need to work and figure this out. They'll reschedule the race soon and we need to make sure those shields don't fail again."

Her boss gave her a concerned look, "Very well. You do well as always. Don't take this event as a reflection of your skills."

5. City of the Clouds

Nate stared at the *Firefly*. It looked comical sitting in the middle of a street with its wings extended. He thought back to his last race. The memories after he hit the safety shield were a blur but he did remember experiencing a sudden unexplainable stall.

"Are you alright?" Nafais asked him.

"Fine," Nate responded. "What happened?"

Nafais didn't respond before Armine spoke up, "You flew rampant through the streets. Nearly killed two of the guards."

Nate caught the glare Nafais shot Armine. He was getting the feeling there was more to the relationship between those two; a far deeper connection then a Captain of the Guard and his Princess. Then again maybe that was normal here. He looked back to the *Firefly*. He began trying to figure how he was going to get the speed needed for takeoff. In front of the aircraft was a set of stairs leading to the palace but behind it, if he could get the aircraft turned around he might be able to get airborne. It would be tricky though.

"What is her name?" Nafais asked.

Mirage

"Firefly," Nate responded without thinking.

"Firefly," Nafais repeated, "What a beautiful name. What kind of creature is she?"

Nate gave her a puzzled look, "It's not a creature. It's a plane. You know a machine for flying..." Nate trailed off as he realized a society with wings on their back had no need for an aircraft, "Never mind."

"A machine for flying? Incredible," Nafais ran her hand along the aircraft's wing. Nate caught Armine's eye's rolling. For some reason, this rubbed Nate the wrong way. Before he could react though Nafais spoke up.

"Are we able to move it away from the market?"

"Yeah, just let me get her going." Nate quickly stepped into the cockpit as the canopy opened. He got settled in before he noticed Nafais watching him. He looked to his side, the designers had added another seat for dual flight races. He looked back to the princess and then to Armine.

"Would you like to join me...uhm...Princess," he asked watching Armine. A flicker of something crossed Armine's face but it was too quick to discern what it was.

"I would be delighted," Nafais replied easily stepping in due to how short the Fire Fly was. Nate went to help her fold her wings into the cockpit. Armine grabbed his arm and pinned it to the aircraft side. Nate let out a yelp of pain as his arm was twisted.

"You will not touch the Princess in that way," Armine stated firmly. There was an almost possessive tone to his voice.

"Relax Captain," Nafais stated as she folded her own wings, "He does not know what he just did. I will explain it to him. Now go and prepare space for *Firefly.*" With that Armine left.

Nate rubbed his arm and didn't bother filtering his speech, "What the hell?!"

Nafais chuckled a little, "Tell me, Nathan, would you simply grab one of my breasts and help me stow it away?"

"Of course not!" Nate responded. He couldn't believe she would think he would do such a thing.

"Then neither should you touch the wings of another," Nafais stated.

Nate felt his eyes widen, "You mean..."

Nafais nodded, "Wings are very sensitive and are not something to be touched by anyone but the owner and his or her lover."

"I'm so sorry!" Nate exclaimed, "I didn't mean anything by it. I was only trying to help."

"Relax Nathan. You did not know. There are quite a few social constructs that revolve around our wings. You might learn them in time but for now, refrain from touching or staring at the wings of another. Now how do you move this creature?"

Nate shook his head. He was going to have to be careful he didn't screw up again. He had a fear that if he did, Armine would take pride in causing him physical harm. Nate shook his head dispelling the thoughts. So far Nafais had shown him no aggression. However, that didn't mean that she was harmless. He reached forward and turned the master switch on, lowering the canopy. The display lit up swirling with colors as the aircraft provided a status report. Nate reviewed it quickly. The aircraft sustained no damage as far as he could tell. He was just taxiing so he omitted the walk around.

"What is all this?" Nafais asked.

"It's the way the *Firefly* talks to me. This control gives information about engines, altitude, heading, flight controls, and so on so I can make decisions while operating it," Nate explained as he went through the engine start procedures.

"And what is it you are doing now?"

Nate paused in his action, noting the interest painted across Nafais' features, "I'm getting the engines ready to start. I need to turn on the electrical, setting the thrust levers to..." Nate trailed off as Nafais' confusion became apparent, "I'm going to move it."

Nafais nodded, "I see." She remained silent as Nate got the engine going. She did, however, comment on the volume of the engine noise. Nate just brushed it off. He opted to use only one engine for the taxi in order to save fuel. He also went through various checks to make sure everything truly was in order before folding the wings back.

"Uhm Na–I mean Princess..." as he did a quick calculation in his head, "I'm not going to have the fuel to get very far." It was true; he had about thirty minutes of fuel left in the *Firefly's* tanks. That wasn't even enough to get from the race track to his hangar.

"Fuel?" Nafais asked.

"Yes. It's what the *Firefly* runs on. Jet-A fuel. Do you know where we can find any?" Nate replied as he maneuvered the aircraft towards Armine.

"So it's like steam?"

"I guess, only it burns."

"I am sure we can find some," Nafais said softly. Nate nodded and let the breaks off allowing the aircraft to roll through the streets.

6. West Wind Flight Track, Safety Command

The safety command of the West Wind Flight Track was abuzz with activity as the race dragged on. Karly glanced from her display to the rest of her command. They still had no idea what had happened to Nate and she worried about it happening again. Since the last race, she had designed and implemented new security measures to keep the pilots and spectators safe. The safety shields were now composed of two layers so if one failed the other would stay operational, in theory. The ring that had caused the accidents last time had been replaced; it was now simply a hologram designed to alert officials if anyone hit it. In retrospect, the design was what they should have had originally but it took an accident with spectators getting injured to get funding for her department.

"Prime the safety shields," she instructed. It was still early in the race but she was watching the two lead aircrafts. They were pulling tight turns in close proximity and she was waiting for one of them to bump the other. She watched them as they rounded another corner and shuddered at the mere inches of separation between the planes. The spectators saw it as amazing aircraft handling, she saw it as why her job was so hard these days.

"Ma'am we have a problem," her second in command called.

"What's wrong?" Karly asked as she used her panel to manipulate the wind currents on the track to eliminate the crosswind. She also increased its speed hoping to slow the speeding aircraft down if only slightly.

"The *Firefly's* transponder is active," her second in command reported.

Karly froze, "What did you just say?"

"*Firefly* is transmitting."

"Where is it?"

"Four miles due east of the race track."

What's east of here? Karly asked herself. The answer was not pleasant, there was nothing, but mountains.

"Prepare to dispatch rescue teams as soon as the race is finished," she ordered. As much as she wanted to send them right away she couldn't afford to have them off site if something happened during the race. *Position before self,* she told herself.

Position before self.

She looked back to the racers. She had turned off the announcer comments for this race but she knew what they were saying. Praising the flying of those pilots as the crowds went wild. Her thoughts, however, stayed on Nate. He was out there and what was she doing? Nothing. If they lost the transponder signal then they might never find him again. If she sent the rescue teams to find him they could very well lose more racers. She sighed.

"Get me a fix on *Firefly's* position," she ordered and managed to divert most of her attention back to the race. It bothered her that Nate was transmitting now, nearly a month after his disappearance.

"They are entering the final turn ma'am," her second in command reported. Kate snapped herself out of her daze.

"Activate the ring," she ordered. She watched from the window as the ring that made up the final obstacle appeared. Brilliant orange columns ascended from the floor of the race track and formed a perfect circle making an ideal replacement for the older model.

Mirage

The racers came careening around the turn, the two lead aircrafts separated by mere feet. She watched as they barrel-rolled together towards the ring.

"They're going to try and make it at the same time," she whispered. No one had ever attempted that. At least this time they wouldn't hit the ring.

"Ma'am somethings wrong with the ring," the second in command called.

"What?"

"Its power output is increasing. At this rate hitting the beams will cause damage when the racers reach it. Kate couldn't believe it. She hadn't even assigned enough power to the holographic generator for that to be possible. She watched the ring closely as it began to glow brighter, red and light blue streaks began to fly through it sporadically. Naturally, the crowd went wild. She had to act quickly.

"Get me the track manager," she directed. She had to get permission to call off the race unless an aircraft was physically damaged.

"Track command," Damion answered.

"The ring is drawing too much power," Karly stated as she reviewed the data. Her heart sank. If the ring kept drawing more power it could short out everything, only this time it could affect the massive engines keeping the race track aloft.

"What's the situation?"

"If it stays like this we'll lose more than just racers," Karly replied. There was no response as the racer neared the ring, "Sir I need authorization to kill the race!" She watched the panel turned red. The engines were in danger of failing. She waited but the authorization never came. When she decided to act it was too late. The two lead aircrafts spiraled into the ring. They were off center. The larger one lost both its wings immediately while the other lost only its vertical stabilizer and one of its horizontal stabilizers. The larger aircraft plowed into the floor. The shields activated automatically. A warning flashed cautioning a fault with their integrity. The other aircraft skidded towards the edge of the track crashing through the weakened shields and into the crowded stands.

Mirage

"Safety Command to all racers! Break Immediately! I say again—" Karly was interrupted by a loud alarm as one of the race track engines failed. The deck pitched drastically as the track began a slow falling spiral. The shift sent some racers careening into the crowd. Explosions erupted along the audience stands killing countless people. "Break! Break! Break!" She yelled into her microphone as another explosion rocked the track. The Safety Command center's windows shattered from the shock wave sending glass everywhere. Alarms blared as lights flashed. The remaining racers quickly flew from the damaged track. Damage reports flew over the radio.

"Sector four engine failure. Track is losing altitude and is unrecoverable."

"Racers clear of track."

"Power dispersal failing."

"Prepare for evacuations," Damion ordered. Kate looked at the display. There was not enough time to evacuate properly. She shut the ring down, scrambling to think of possible ways to save the track. She had an epiphany.

"Get everyone inside. I'll divert power from external shields," she called over the radio and set to work. What she was going to do was risky. The track had large external shields around it to maintain breathable air at high altitudes. If she cut the power there might be enough undamaged power supply to keep the track airborne. The disadvantage was any spectators on the stands wouldn't be able to breathe. They would all need to retreat to the pressurized lower decks.

"Karly I can't authorize–" Her boss began.

"I'm not asking permission," Karly interrupted as she put on an oxygen mask. She cut the shields. More alarms blared as the air thinned. She skillfully manipulated the control diverting the power.

"Command get those engines going," she ordered.

"Engines coming online," a reply came. Although the spiral continued the track decent slowed. Every possible alarm in Karly's command was going off, her computer was screaming at her to do something to restore the air supply. She could only hope that all the spectators were inside the pressurized parts of the track. Then the descent halted abruptly and the spin began to slow.

"Attention all units. Track has been stabilized. We are descending for repairs. Please reduce all power consumption to a minimum."

Karly let out a sigh of relief and shut off her panel. She looked at her second in command.

"Excellent job ma'am."

"Thank you."

"You know you just lost your job, right?" he asked.

Kate nodded, "Take care of my race track for me."

7. City of the Clouds

Armine walked down the halls of the palace, his face showing no emotion as was normal for a guard on patrol. His mind, however, was buzzing with activity. He should have been looking for every possible threat; instead, he was thinking of Nafais. He couldn't believe that she had rejected him, sort of. He knew her well enough that it seemed unlikely that she would agree to be his, though. He let out a sigh as he admired a statue of the Princess of the Sky. Her large beautiful wings held out to their full length. He felt his own wings rustle slightly but quickly regained control of them before he caused a scene.

However, Nafais made the act pointless as she grabbed him with her wings and shoved him into a room. She closed the door and turned towards him. Armine's heart began to race as possible scenarios ran through his head. However, fact rang through even his most exotic thoughts.

"Nafais!" he hissed, "Do you know what people will think of you for that action!"

Nafais waved a dismissive hand in the small room, "I have bigger problems. Do you know what fuel is?"

Mirage

Armine tilted his head, "What?"

"Nathan needs *fuel* for *Firefly.* It's what it eats, I think, but I can't find anyone who knows what it is," Nafais explained.

Armine rubbed his forehead. Of course, Nafais was worried about the human, and it was all she worried about lately, "No I don't. I do think we need to talk though."

"Figures," Nafais grumbled as her wings fell.

"Princess I need to speak with you," Armine tried again. Nafais head shot up.

"Formalities? In private? What gives Armine?" she asked.

"This conversation is very important to me Princess. I need you to hear me out."

"Okay, but stop calling me Princess. It creeps me out how you change your demeanor so quickly," Nafais responded as her wings rustled, signalling her curiosity. "What's on your mind Captain?"

"I offered you a proposition on the day of the race. I wish to make good on those words," Armine stated. He felt a nervousness stirring inside him. He knew he feared rejection but he also longed for her answer, good or bad. Nafais's eyes fell. She reached a hand out and placed it on his arm.

"Armine, I don't know if we should."

Armine sighed, "Why not? We've known each other so long Nafais."

Nafais shook her head, "I want to Armine. I had been thinking of it before the race but what if something happened. I can't bear to lose you as a friend."

Armine shook his head, "I would never abandon you Nafais."

"I know that," Nafais said softly, "It's me I'm worried about."

Armine's mind raced, trying to comprehend what Nafais was saying. Why would she be worried about her doing something? She was a Princess. They hardly did anything wrong. It was then that he had the idea that maybe she thought he loved the façade she put on and not the real Nafais.

"Nafais–" Armine was abruptly cut off as the door burst open. Nafais let out shriek and Armine raised his wings defensively in front of the Princess while reaching for his blade.

"Uhm..." a very nervous looking messenger began, "Captain Armine, Princess Nafais, there has been a development in the market that the Queen wishes' both of you see it."

"What kind of development?" Nafais asked, peering over Armine's wing.

"One concerning the human," the messenger replied simply before flying off. Armine let out a sigh.

Nafais giggled, "Oh, when my mother hears the rumors..."

"It will be nothing good for either of us," Armine finished for her before they both dissolved into laughter, "Shall we?"

Nafais looked hesitant, "You know Armine I could get used to being protected by your wings."

Armine's wings shot out stiff as boards, "My lady, I must urge you that we make our way to the market."

Nafais laughed as she walked past Armine, "So you like the idea of protecting me, do you?" Armine shook his head. "Or is it the idea that I would be yours to protect?"

Armine cursed under his breath as he fought for control over his wings. Nafais always knew how to push his buttons but it was dangerous when she played with these new influences she had.

They reached the market without further events. Nathan joined them quickly as they surveyed the scene. Three large objects had crashed through the marketplace taking out various merchant stands and leaving smoking trails behind them. When Armine knelt next to one of the objects it appeared scalding hot.

"What's that smell?" Nafais asked, holding a sleeve of her white gown to her nose. Armine took a sniff and felt the scent burn his nose.

"That's fuel," Nate replied as he looked at a smaller third object.

Doesn't smell natural, Armine thought to himself. It made him wonder why they would need something that foul smelling, and what would eat such a material. He watched as Nathan examined each object. Armine was not too pleased with the human's appearance, even less pleased that he was tasked with helping the creature return home. He had real work to do after all. It didn't help that it had been Nafais that asked him for the help. *She will be my undoing*, he mused.

"What are they, Nathan?" Nafais asked.

"Those look like parts of wings and this is a vertical stabilizer," Nate explained. Both Nafais and Armine locked his eyes with uncomprehending stares, "Uhm...the straight up and down fin on the back of *Firefly.*"

"Oh," Nafais replied as she looked at the pieces of what Armine assumed to be a creature. It was strange to him that there was no blood anywhere. Or the fact that only part of the creature had appeared unlike the *Firefly's* dramatic appearance during the race. "What do the letters N, G, O, H, E mean?"

"November Golf Oscar Hotel Echo," Nate muttered.

How he got a month and the name of a boarding establishment out of the letters was beyond Armine.

"I know that racer. They are call signs. Controllers use them to I.D the plane they are talking to over the radio. That plane's name is *Claw's Breath.*"

"Appealing," Armine remarked.

"It was behind me when I hit the shields," Nate stated.

Armine sighed and left Nafais and Nathan to look at the damage. He had more important things to do.

"Captain Armine?" Nafais called.

Stopping dead in his tracks, Armine spun to face her, "Yes Princess?"

"I require assistance in my chambers this evening. Would you be able to join me?"

Armine fought to keep his wings under control as he dipped slightly into a bow, "It would be my honor Princess."

8. City of the Clouds

Nate walked through the grand halls into the throne room. He had been summoned by the Queen and with Nafais off doing who knows what on her own and Armine attending to his guard duty he was left alone to face the head of their government.

"Nathan, I trust your stay with us has been agreeable?" the Queen's gentle voice questioned as he approached her. Nate hesitated then quickly bowed. He heard the Queen laugh slightly, "Thank you. Now how are my daughter and Captain Armine treating you?"

Nate shrugged, "Nafais is great but I get the feeling Armine has other things on his mind. Especially since it's been weeks since I got here."

The Queen nodded, "Yes other *things* indeed."

Nate looked at the Queen tilting his head, "So you think so too?"

The Queen returned his gaze, "I do not know of what you speak."

Nate rolled his eyes, "Nafais does that too when she's lying."

"Another trait she has inherited," the Queen chuckled dryly, "Now what is it you think is going on?"

"Armine has it bad for Nafais," Nate responded bluntly then flinched. He considered that maybe that was not the best thing to tell the monarch; maybe he had gotten a little too used to them in the past month or so. "Uhm...what I mean is that...the Captain of the Guard...has a...uhm...infatuation with your daughter. I guess, maybe...I could be completely...likely am wrong."

The Queen's face showed no emotional reaction, "Relax Nathan. It is not why I summoned you. Though it is good to know. I will deal with it on another occasion. Right now, I need to speak to you about the *Firefly.*"

Nate let out a sigh of relief, "What do you need to know?"

"Fuel," the Queen said simply.

"Uhm...okay," Nate replied, "She runs on Jet-A fuel. It's a fossil fuel, made by years of compressing organic matter in the ground and then refined somehow. Nafais said you guys had some to fill her up."

The Queen nodded, "We do not. Nafais assumed you spoke of the steam we produce by magic as that is how everything is powered in our city. I know not what this ground is of which you speak. It is only legend. We have never come across it to my knowledge. I am sure my mystics can find a way to get you what you need though."

Nate didn't say anything. He was disappointed that Nafais' word hadn't been what he thought it would be. But at the same time, it didn't surprise him. In retrospect, he should have known as he had not seen any ground anywhere near the city. The Queen lead Nate to a balcony that overlooked the city center. The sun was setting, reflecting off clouds and turning the sky into a beautiful display of reds and oranges. Below them, silently waiting, was the *Firefly*.

The Queen sighed, "Beautiful isn't it?" Nate nodded, "I must confess something to you, Nathan. I am quite enthralled with you and your *bird* as Nafais says you call it. More so than I like and it brings me great pain to think that one day I may not be able to look out upon its majestic body." Nate wasn't quite sure how to take that, "Now I must show you something...I am sorry but I feel you must see it." The Queen raised her hand and an image shimmered to life, showing a race on the West Wind Flight Track.

"Wow, that's where I'm from. How can I get there from here?" Nate stared as he watched the racers fly, the image looked so real.

"These are events from earlier today. My mystics and I were able to get just a small glimpse into your world. I warn you it is not a pretty sight."

"What do you mean?" Nate asked as the racers made the final turn and headed for what appeared to be a newly designed ring. The Queen didn't need to answer as the racers collided with the ring. Nate watched as they crashed and as an explosion rocked the race track. He fixated on the windows of the safety command as they shattered.

"Karly," he whispered. The race track fell into a descending spiral before the image vanished, "No! What happened?"

Mirage

"I do not know. Even our combined power would not allow for a longer glimpse."

"What do you mean you don't know? You're supposed to know everything aren't you?" Nate snapped angrily.

"Have you noticed that Armine's wings are black while the rest of us, excluding my daughter, hold light colored wings?" The Queen asked.

"That has got to be the worst transition to a new subject ever," Nate grumbled, "Of course I have. I haven't given it much thought though. Still getting used to the idea of you all having wings."

"Armine comes from a dark line. I found him as a child, abandoned. His father was a Captain in the Royal Guard. He was exiled after he killed his entire family, save Armine, in cold blood. He and his mistress vowed revenge on the city, and especially on myself and my daughter. He is now commanding a cloud schooner called the *Mirage*. For the most part, he stays away from the city but I worry that he may try to take it by force."

Nate nodded, not sure where the Queen was going with this.

"We've known of your world longer then I've let on. Armine's father was...entranced by Karly, Claiming she would build a gate-way that would bring them together."

"Gate-way?" Nate asked. He could sense that the Queen was choosing her words carefully, "My sister makes safety systems for the race track."

"You were brought here were you not?" the Queen remarked.

"But I hit safety shields. They were never designed to..." Nate trailed off, "Would a Gate-way give off a lot of radiation?"

The Queen shook her head, "It would give off magic."

"What can measure magic?" Nate asked.

The Queen thought for a moment, "Anything really."

"So something that detects radiation could pick up magic?"

"It would be possible, whatever this radiation you speak of might be," the Queen replied.

Mirage

Nate sat heavily onto a near by chair, "She built a gate-way and didn't even know it."

"I beg your pardon?"

"Karly. The shields she designed. We thought they gave off radiation so we weren't able to keep them up long, but there was an unexplained lack of exposure effects from the repeated use of the shields. If the sensors were picking up magic..."

"Then when it reached a high enough level you were allowed to pass through," the Queen finished.

"Is my sister in danger?"

"I wish I had an answer for you dear Nathan," the Queen replied. Nate nodded, bowed and turned to leave.

"Nathan wait," the Queen called. Nate turned back, "I meant what I said about being enthralled by you and your machine. Perhaps you would accompany me to my chamber to...further my understanding of the *Firefly?*"

9. City of the Clouds

Nafais paced nervously around her chamber. Normally she would be on her balcony watching the sun as it descended through the sky towards the horizon that never seemed to exist. Today was different. She had prepared everything: her candles illuminated the room with a soft glow, she had made sure that the environment was as inviting as possible.

"Why did you invite him to your chambers?" she asked herself out loud, "You could have gone for a walk in the castle grounds, a flight under the moonlight but no, you had to get his hopes up and invite him to your chambers."

You know why you invited him to your chambers, her mind informed her.

"I wanted to discuss his offer, but I should not do it here."

You want him just as much as he wants you, her mind pressed.

"I just don't want to lose him," she muttered.

You won't.

Mirage

"I can't be sure though," she defended. Armine didn't know it yet but she was going to live a lot longer than he was. There was a way for someone who loved an immortal to live as long as they do but it meant giving themselves fully to the other. Would he do that for her? Would she even want him to? There was so much about Armine she didn't know, like why his wings were black for starters. She flicked her wings trying to dispel her nervous energy. Armine would never intentionally hurt her but his passing would be devastating to her.

Would it not be better to have loved and have to lose them than live forever alone? She asked herself. Before she could answer she heard a knock on her door. She quickly straightened her robe and tucked her wings neatly onto her back. She confidently opened the door to see exactly who she expected. What made her breath hitch was that Armine did not appear as she expected. He was adorned in his guard uniform, weapons and all. The gold-plated metal shone beautifully in the candlelight and Nafais felt her wings rise slightly in interest from the sight. His large black wings looked freshly preened as they rustled on his back.

"You asked to see me, Princess," he stated. She nodded and let him inside. Armine removed his helmet and placed it on a table in Nafais's room while Nafais forced her wings against her back. There was no need to show Armine she thought he was attractive, not now anyway.

"You cleaned up," Armine observed.

"Well, I couldn't have the Captain of the Guard..." Nafais trailed off as Armine looked at her. There was a sadness inside his eyes, an almost pleading look that was begging her to stop torturing him. "Armine I'm sorry. I should have given you an answer as soon as you asked me."

Armine waved a hand, his wings dropping slightly, "It's alright Nafais. I was a fool for trying."

"No," Nafais protested, "You don't understand Armine. My mother and I...we are immortals."

Armine raised an eyebrow, "I grew up with you Nafais."

Nafais nodded, her own wings relaxing to rest on the ground, "Yes you did...but I will not die with you. Armine my mother loved my father. His death, though premature, tore her apart. I don't know if I can handle it."

"I would suggest not living in fear of what could be," Armine stated, "But you have always known what's best for yourself Nafais. Do as you please," he sighed heavily, "I will remain by your side as a friend for as long as I can." Nafais felt tears welling up in her eyes. She loved him so much, but couldn't allow it to grow any deeper. They had known each other for so long, he was the perfect mate, strong, distinguished and honorable. Her mother would approve despite the pain it might cause Nafais.

A hand lifted Nafais' chin, "I understand Nafais," Armine said softly.

"No Armine you do not..." Nafais whispered as the hand left her. Armine turned towards the door.

"I bid you goodnight Princess," Armine said. There it was again—that sudden change into a guard's demeanor. Nafais wanted to call for him to stop but as he walked towards her door she couldn't get her mouth to work. Her mind raced with how to get him to stay, her wings weren't long enough to grab him and she wasn't fast enough to put herself between him and the ever-closer door. She frantically looked at the offending object and remembered the ceremonial staff flanking its frame. If only she had the control over the magic her mother did. Her control over the wind wouldn't be enough to move them.

Armine was about to reach the door when Nafais felt the magic that only her mother and the mystics were able to control surge build inside her. She had to stop Armine; this was the only way. She felt the magic surge through her core seconds before a sharp pain ran through her body; she let out a scream.

10. City of the Clouds

Armine was just reaching for the door when a burst of cold light-blue magic crossed the staff in front of him blocking his path. At Nafais' scream of pain he didn't hesitate. In one smooth motion, he drew his sword and turned to face whoever was attacking his Princess. He found no aggressor, only Nafais collapsed on the floor rubbing her head. He felt his heart stop as he quickly rushed to her side.

"Nafais what happened?" he asked. Though he had a pretty good idea. Nafais had told him about what happened if a being who was never meant to wield magic managed to channel it. Their bodies couldn't cope with the magic and it normally caused a searing pain worse than anything they would ever experience. It was a contingency that ensured only certain beings could control it. It looked like Nafais was one of the unlucky few that could summon magic but were never meant to use it.

"Don't go," Nafais pleaded, tears running down her face, "Please don't go. I'm so sorry."

Armine gripped Nafais' hand and helped her to her bed, "I'm right here. Don't worry. I will call for a surgeon."

Nafais shook her head, "Please Armine forgive me. I would be honored to be your woman."

Armine felt his heart skip a beat, "But what of your immortality?"

"I would suffer for all eternity if it meant not losing you sooner than necessary," Nafais replied. He felt her multi-colored wings surround him and pull him down on top of her. Their primary feathers brushed against each other in a lovers' embrace.

"Nafais," A blush colored Armine's face.

"Would you preen my wings?" Nafais asked in a whisper.

Armine fought for control over his wings but at last, he lost. They shot straight out forcing Nafais to part her wings. If the princess minded, she did not show it.

"You have such magnificent wings," she murmured as she ran her hands down his feathers. Armine shivered.

"What has gotten into you Nafais?" he asked. He tried to get up but the Princess held him. It was then that he remembered another side effect of being joined with magic for the first time. It could remove one's inhibitions more effectively then alcohol.

Mirage

"I have always wanted to feel your feathers under my fingers," Nafais said wistfully.

Armine sighed, he could not take advantage of her in this state, "Nafais, let me up."

"Why?" Nafais asked.

"I must find your mother. She can help your altered state."

Nafais shook her head, a little hurt showing behind her eyes, "But...do you not want me?"

Armine fought to get his wings down and extricated himself form Nafais, "I want the Nafais I grew up with, not one I can take from what I please."

Nafais nodded, "I'm sorry Armine."

Armine nodded, "I will return. Till then stay here." Armine quickly left and let out a heavy sigh. The magic may have loosened up Nafais but as soon as the Queen brought her back to normal, she would be the same, and he would have lost his only chance with her.

11. City of the Clouds

Nate walked quietly down the dark halls of the palace. He had just come from the Queen's personal chambers. She had proven quite interested in the *Firefly*. They had spoken for hours about it and how it flew. He supposed it made sense, the Queen would like to know what was in her Kingdom.

Or is it Queendom? Nate mused to himself as he stopped to look out an archway. The city was truly beautiful but it seemed even more so bathed in the silver light of the moon. Nate found himself growing quite fond of it even in the short time he had been there. Not just the city but he was growing quite fond of the Queen as well. He felt a slight pressure and light pain spread through his back but he dismissed it.

He sighed and surveyed the rooftops. That's when he noticed movement on top of a few buildings. He looked closer thinking they may be stargazers but something wasn't right. As he watched the figures, they were slinking along the rooftops, almost all black and barely visible. He followed their path and noticed they were heading right for the Queen's chambers. He felt worry weigh down his stomach as the figures took to the air and disappeared into the night. He looked around and noticed two guards on patrol. He ran to them.

"Guards! The Queen's in danger."

The guards turned quickly, "Be careful of what you speak human. That is a grave claim you are making."

"I'm telling you I saw something and it's going for the Queen," Nate argued. If he was truthful the only thing really backing his story was his gut feeling that something bad was going to happen but he wasn't about to tell the guards that.

"Well, then, that something will be dealt with. Now on with you. We have real work to do."

"Humor me," Nate demanded. The guards raised an eyebrow, "I am ordering you as a charge of Princess Nafais to check in on the Queen."

The guards sighed but complied. Nate smiled to himself having manipulated the government system in this city effectively. They reached the chambers and one of the guards knocked. There was no answer.

"My Queen. We are here under the direction of Nathan. Are you there?" one of the guards called. He looked at the other when no answer came, the worry beginning to show on his face. The two guards wasted no time and burst into the chambers. Inside was a mess. Tables, books, scrolls, chairs, and everything else was strewn across the floor and a window had been broken. Nate felt the pit in his stomach grow. The stiffness and pain in his back returning. He walked to the balcony as he heard the guards discussing.

"We must find Captain Armine."

"He is with the Princess."

"The disappearance of the Queen is of higher importance then their childhood dalliance do you not think?" As the guards bickered Nate scanned the skies. Surely if they kidnapped her, they would take her by flight. He was rewarded by the occasional glimpse of a light-colored wing in the darkness. He turned to tell the guards but they flew past him before he could.

"The Queen is that way! They're getting away!" he called after them but got no response. He began to fidget, feeling the pain in his back growing. He couldn't just do nothing. He looked around for a way to help. If he let them go much longer they would be too far to track. His eyes settled on the *Firefly*. Her radar could track them and her speed could run them down. He didn't hesitate. He ran down to her.

Once there he stepped inside and began to start the engines. He had never felt so slow in his life. Finally, after what felt like hours the engines spun up. He taxied in line with a street and noticed a huge flaw in his plan. There was nowhere long enough for a takeoff roll. He looked around and noticed the edge of the city. As far as he knew they were thousands of feet up if there was even a ground.

What the hell? Why not? he thought to himself as he lined up the *Firefly*. He pushed the throttles to takeoff power and held the breaks as the engines spooled up. Once at full power, he released the breaks and took off like a shot. The aircraft used up the "runway" length quickly and plunged off the city's edge. Alarms blared warning Nate of the ineffective flight pattern. He threw the wing sweep controls forward to gain as much lift as possible and prayed it worked. After a few seconds, his airspeed increased to a sufficient level and he eased himself out of the dive. He sighed in relief as he turned towards where he last saw the glimpse of the Queen's wing. His collision avoidance radar showed a group of five figures up ahead.

Now, what do I do? He asked himself as he closed the gap between them. He had no weapons and he couldn't very well just go supersonic and fly over them. The pressure wave would kill the Queen. He felt a panic return to him. He felt if he didn't get to the Queen it would end him. Then a thought occurred to him. He knew how to fit the *Firefly* through the toughest of obstacles. If he could position himself so his wing would hit the wings of the kidnappers then he might be able to do some real damage. As he approached the group he rolled into a knife edge and extended his wings forward. He watched the group carefully and managed to slam his right wingtip into one of the men holding the Queen.

"Warning starboard wing contact." The computer cautioned. Nate paid it no mind as he circled back. He saw the man he hit spiralling out of control and the Queen rolling out of a dive. She beat her large wings escaping the grasp of her assailant. Nate slammed his other wing into two of her attackers as they attempted to chase after her. He rolled himself into a climb before turning back.

Three down two to go, he thought to himself. He flew after the Queen assuming the others would show themselves when they went for her. Up ahead he could see guards from the City of Clouds coming towards them. He then saw his targets. He had no idea what had gotten into him. Normally the idea of killing or harming anyone was appalling to him. But now he felt that these men, who had attacked Armine's Queen, Nafais's mother deserved to die. He slid between the Queen and the pursuers. Taking both out with his tail. The hit cost him though as his rudder jammed.

"Warning rudder failure." The computer called. Nate wrestled with the controls but couldn't keep the nose down. It rose, the aircraft stalled and then slipped into a spin.

12. City of the Clouds

Armine flew as fast as he could toward his Queen. How could these villains slip through the city's defense undetected? It seemed impossible yet they had done it. It was time to upgrade them. The Queen soon came into view along with something else he never expected. He watched as the *Firefly* pulled what should have been an impossible maneuver and use its wings to basically cut two of the assailent in half. He watched it as it then rolled away. He had never thought Nathan to be a killer. Especially not in this way. He was pulled from his thoughts as he and the rest of the guards formed a protective formation around the Queen. He heard the roar of the *Firefly* as it flew past. He looked just in time to see it take out two more chasing attackers.

"Unbelievable," he muttered. The Queen hovered in flight and turned to watch the *Firefly*.

"He is remarkable," she whispered. Much to Armine's displeasure, the Queen refused to move as an expression of dread graced her features in the moonlight.

"What is it my Queen?" he asked.

"He…I fear Nathan cannot recover," she responded. Armine looked and sure enough, the *Firefly* looked to be spinning around one wing in a steep dive.

"I'm sure he will be fine my Queen. Now we must return you to the palace." The Queen still would not move until she saw Nathan pull out of his stunt. Armine growled to himself. Surely that human was just showing off. Then the *Firefly* flew over them at breakneck speed towards the castle. Armine's eyes followed. It was tipping its wings as if encouraging them to follow. Realization hit Armine like a ton of bricks. He had sent most of the guards out looking for the Queen and left Nafais undefended.

"We are returning to the palace now," he ordered as the guards forced the Queen to move. Armine didn't wait for them. He shot forward towards the tower which contained Nafais' chambers. The light was still on in the room but it meant very little. The *Firefly* circled the tower flying back to Armine. He willed his wings to beat faster. His muscles burned and his breath was comming in short heavy gasps by the time he touched down on Nafais' balcony. He heard the sounds of a struggle coming from inside. He looked to see his other guards and the Queen rapidly gaining on him but they were still too far away. He had to act. Armine drew his blade and rushed through the curtains obscuring the inside of Nafais's chambers. Inside he was greeted with a shocking sight. Nafais was pulling a dagger from one man's chest. She swung around. Her wings extending as she took to the air lunging for another attacker. She grabbed one of the two remaining men by his wing and sliced downwards cutting it off at the joint. She used him as leverage and pushed off him, sending him out an open window and her towards the last man. She grabbed him and they struggled. Armine stood stupefied as he watched Nafais fight. He never knew her to be trained so well.

She swung herself onto the man's shoulders, using her wings for balance and sliced her blade through the man's throat. They fell to the ground together. In a moment all was silent except for Nafais's heavy breathing. Slowly she rose to her feet and faced Armine.

"Enjoy the show?" she asked with distaste in her voice. It was that moment Armine realized he had been staring, and his wings were rustling. He forced them down, the blood rushing to his face, "You need to...to be more effective in delegating guards," Nafais remark, her breathing heavier than normal.

"I would agree," the Queen said from behind him, "There is no circumstance that would warrant leaving my daughter undefended."

"My Queen we were searching for you," Armine defended.

"Yet it was Nathan who was my savior not you," the Queen replied. Her voice cold as ice.

"Nathan?" Nafais asked. At that moment *Firefly's* roar filled the room. Nafais and the Queen rushed outside and watched the twin lights of its tail speed away.

"What are those lights?" a guard asked.

"If my understanding is correct it is the result of the fuel's combustion," the Queen replied. Armine cocked an eyebrow. How did the Queen suddenly know this?

"Fuel?" Nafais whispered, "You mean what it eats?"

The Queen nodded, "That is correct my daughter. Nathan has proven quite capable with his steed."

"Mother, he was low on fuel. He said he wouldn't have very much flight time left."

"How long has he been airborne?" Armine asked, grasping that the *Firefly* would need to eat soon or it would fall from the sky.

"I fear too long," Nafais responded. They watched as the silver *Firefly* circled back towards them. The distant roar it made was not as pronounced as it once had been. Then as it passed it fell silent.

13. City of the Clouds

Nafais felt her heart drop. She saw dread spread across her mother's face. "Why doesn't he get down?"

"Because he needs space. He can't hover like we can," her mother explained.

"How do you know so much about this creature?" Armine asked.

"Nathan and I discussed it at length earlier today," the queen explained, "Captain Armine quickly, clear our longest street." Nafais watched as Armine nodded and took to the sky.

"Are you alright mother?" Nafais asked when they were alone.

"I will be better once Nathan is safe. And you my daughter? You are an impressive fighter."

Nafais blushed, "Fine. I guess Armine's rubbing off on me."

"So it would seem," the Queen replied, "Come, we must greet my savior." With that, they took to the air towards the longest street. Nafais watched a silent *Firefly* as she glided through the air on motionless wings. The problem was it wasn't heading towards the area being cleared, it was heading for the marketplace. Nafais and her mother landed at the foot of the stairwell and watch as it approached. Nafais was expecting a nice dignified and graceful landing. What she saw was nothing of the sort. The *Firefly* dipped a wing and began to lose height rapidly as its nose turned away from its direction of travel, then only meters above the street it straightened out and its wings extended forward as the nose raised. It eased down towards the ground. Before its feet hit though, a shower of sparks erupted as it struck its tail. It slammed itself down onto its feet, bounced up before falling back to the street and started to skid. It was much like the first landing of a child who ended up on his back. Only *Firefly* didn't roll. She skidded around her nose, her wing grabbing the ground and spinning it into merchant stands. Nafais felt Armine's wings wrap around her and pull her out of the way as *Firefly* went skidding past.

Once she regained her bearings Nafais looked at Armine, "Making up for your mistake," she teased. It didn't matter that he had left her; she could never be angry with him really. Even though she still felt apprehensive.

Mirage

"Nathan!" the Queen called. Everyone looked at a beaten *Firefly* half buried in debris. The Queen shook off her guards and, closely followed by Nafais and Armine, they approached the battered beast. Its head opened and a ladder extended from its side as Nathan crawled out. He had a bleeding gash on his head and looked to be cradling one of his arms. Nathan never touched the ground. He was swept up in the Queen's wings. Nafais shot her mother a look but the woman didn't seem to notice.

Armine smiled a little, "Some...interesting flying Nathan."

Nathan nodded, "Don't have guns...was the best I could do."

"Your best was beyond that of my guards," the Queen compliment, "Come, you shall spend the night in my chambers. I will get a surgeon to attend to your wounds."

"Mother," Nafais protested.

"Relax daughter. I will not be accompanying him. Nor will Armine accompany you," the Queen stated. Nafais felt her eyes widen. *Her mother knew?*

"I bid you goodnight," the Queen continued, "Captain Armine?"

"Yes, my Queen."

"Make another mistake like tonight and I shall take your wings."

14. City of the Clouds

Nathan awoke to rays of sunlight piercing through his eyelids. He groaned and tried to pull the covers over his head but his dislocated shoulder protested, reminding him of yesterday's events. He slowly opened his eyes and sighed heavily. His sleep had been better than expected, though his aching back had made his rest fitful. It seemed that every time he closed his eyes all he could see were those men with broken wings falling to their deaths and the Queen's worried expression as she brought him to bed. He may have saved the Queen but he felt had forever condemned his soul for taking those lives.

Why did I need to save the Queen? he asked himself. He hadn't questioned it before, attributing it to adrenaline. But he couldn't answer why he had had the need to protect the Queen. Even back home he was no military man. He only ever really looked out for himself and Karly, but now he had damaged the *Firefly* and used all its remaining fuel to save this woman he barely knew. And he had likely stranded himself here away from Karly as a result. He groaned and rolled over ignoring the protests from his back. This was just one big mess.

"Ah, Nathan you are awake," a soft voice came from the balcony. Nate nodded and slowly sat up. He felt his head begin to spin, and he was quickly pushed down by a soft wing, "Stay in bed. You hit your head on your landing. I fear you may need a few days to recover."

Nate nodded and let himself lay back down on the mattress, "What was that last night?"

The Queen seemed to hesitate before responding, "That was...very heroic of you last night." There was a long pause before she continued, "You remember me talking of Armine's dark blood lines?"

"Yah."

"Those were... a kind of relative of his. The *Mirage* creates a crew that mirrors its Captain's soul. I fear that the *Mirage* is close by. Guards are searching for it now."

"You going to tell Armine?" Nate asked.

The Queen shook her head.

"You should know he is going to wonder why all the dead bodies have black wings."

"Yes...my daughter was very skilled last night," the Queen mumbled.

"Nafais...I mean the Princess fought? I'm impressed."

"She should not have needed to," the Queen grumbled, "Armine left her undefended."

Nate decided it would be best if he didn't pursue that avenue of conversation; instead, he opted for a question that had of late been bugging him. "What do I call you?"

The resentment faded from the Queen's face, "You call me as you wish. I am not your Queen so if you would prefer you may address me by my name, Rosaria."

"Ro...Ro...Rosa it is then," Nate said.

Rosa smiled, "I finally think I know who you are. I had been waiting for your return ever since the day we lost you." Nate arched an eyebrow. Rosa extended her wings and laid them out as if presenting them to Nathan, "My King."

15. West Wind Flight Track Loading Dock

Karly looked at the race track. She watched as it slowly rotated upwards back towards its operating altitude. She hadn't been fired as she had expected, only suspended. Turns out firing the person responsible for saving countless lives would be a public relations nightmare for the track. She rolled her eyes at the thought. She stayed watching the track ascend till it disappeared into the cloud layer.

"Just a few weeks," she muttered to herself. Damion had seen to it that she really wasn't missing anything so at least no one would die in her absence. She turned on her heels and walked towards the bus stop. It was going it be a long few weeks. She would likely need a temporary job seeing as she was suspended without pay. She never reached the bus stop as two hands grabbed her shoulders. She let out a cry of surprise but no one was around to hear her. The hands pulled her into the sky. She fought against her attacker and managed to get free of his hold. Only now she was falling.

Great thinking, she scolded herself. She braced herself for the impact as the ground sped up to meet her. Just before she hit, hands once again grabbed her.

Mirage

"Can't have you dying Mistress, now can we?" the attacker said in a deep voice. Karly craned her neck to get a look at him. What she saw made her freeze. He was a big bearded man with a lopsided grin and two black wings. Her mind reeled, unable to form a coherent thought as they climbed above the cloud layer, causing her to lose all ability to fight. Once she finally regained control of her faculties another sight came into view that threatened to grind her mind to a halt once more. Ahead was a pure white ship with brilliant golden sails sailing across the grey clouds. Its appearance was even more mystical due to the contrast of it's bleached white hull against the water-logged clouds. Karly was dropped onto the deck of the ship much to the pleasure of the seemingly all-male crew.

"Look what we have here," one of the men with a large scare on his arm chuckled, "Has the maiden finally rejoined us?"

Karly stared wide-eyed at the men around her. She was standing on a ship, sailing across the clouds. Only one word escaped her lips, "Impossible."

"Iris!" a joyous voice called from the stern of the ship. Karly turned to see a man dressed in a long sky-blue coat and pure charcoal black wings climbing up from the ship's lower decks. "Sorry, it's Karly in this realm is it not? I trust my men were diligent in rescuing you?"

Karly couldn't even bring herself to speak—this was all so surreal. She began to feel like she was spinning and grabbed onto one of the ship's masts for support. "I don't understand," she whispered. She felt a hand on her shoulder as the man in the blue coat pulled her into a hug.

"Did that Queen mess with your mind? No worry my sweet for it will heal with time. Till then welcome aboard my ship, the *Mirage.*"

Karly pushed the winged man away, "What the hell are you talking about? And who are you?" A chuckle rose from the crew but was quickly silenced by a stare from the man who had hugged her. She turned to run but was caught by the arm.

"You used to call me Shadow," the man whispered softly. "Come I will explain everything in my cabin. Emile! Make sail for the portal."

Mirage

"Yes Captain," another man with dark grey wings responded. Shadow led Karly down below deck and secured them in a cabin.

"Okay, what's going on?" Karly demanded.

"I am bringing you home Karly," Shadow explained.

"In the flying Dutchman," Karly muttered, "How is this even possible?"

Shadow cocked his head to one side, "You truly don't remember anything?" Karly shook her head, "Karly you built the *Mirage*."

16. City of the Clouds

"King!?" Nate shouted and jumped out of bed. He lost his balance though and fell back onto the bed, on top of the Queen's presented wings. He quickly remembered the conversation he had had with Nafais about wings and scampered off the bed onto the floor.

Rosa retracted her wings folding them against her back, "I know it must come as a shock..."

"You think!" Nate snapped, "What do you even mean by that?"

"I mentioned Armine's father to you the other day," Rosa said.

Nate rolled his eyes, "Yes and how he's this big bad guy and is the Captain of this dark ship."

"Actually, the *Mirage* is quite the lovely white–"

"Get to the point Rosa!" Nate interrupted. If the Queen was bothered by him overstepping his bounds she did not show it.

"He may have been the one who murdered his family, but his mistress was worse. She built the *Mirage* as an infiltrating attack vessel. I do not know the whole story but I do know I exiled

both..." Rosa trailed off slightly, cupping Nate's face in her hands,

"And lost you along with it."

"No Nafais said her father died in a flying accident," Nate

argued. "And my parents died in a car crash."

Rosa shook her head; her eyes seemed to glisten with

unshed tears, "You volunteered to escort them to the world you

now call home, but you never returned. I don't know what

happened to you to make you forget or to make you lose your

wings, but I do know that Armine's father escaped. Only to steal the

Mirage from my port later on."

Nate shook his head to try and sort through the jumble of

thoughts running through it, "You used my world as a prison?"

"Of sorts...I did not know much of it but it seemed a safe a

place as any to exile those that did not belong here," Rosa replied.

"Who did you exile?"

"The one you call your sister."

Nate's eyes grew wide, "Karly would never–"

"She did Nathan. Look into your memories. She is not the Karly you know. That is a persona imposed upon her by magic that will hold only till she returns to this world. And now she's built a portal between our worlds which will allow her to escape. I would not be surprised if she was on the *Mirage* right now."

"No!" Nathan shouted and quickly bolted from the room. As childish as it might have been it seemed to be the rational thing to do. He ran down and through the streets to the wrecked *Firefly*. It still sat buried in rubble from its rough landing. The area had been cordoned off so he was alone.

As a result, he felt comfortable breaking down. How dare the Queen accuse Karly of such things? Tears streamed down his face as memories of his sister flashed through his mind. She was always supportive, always there for him. Now the memories became tinted with the fact that she may have been plotting against him all these years. The pain in his back grew as he fought to figure out a solution. Much to his dismay the longer he dwelled the less he could remember. Slowly distant memories of Karly began to fade.

Mirage

The Queen's words rang in his ears, *exiled...a persona imposed upon her by magic.* Nate clenched his fists. He fought to feel the pain of loss or betrayal but everything felt numb.

The more he thought about it the more his recent actions made sense. He could never explain why he had felt the need to sacrifice what little fuel he had left in the *Firefly* to save the Queen, and he could never explain why he had suddenly decided to kill those men. He also had no actual memory of his parents. Only a sense of loss regarding them. If he was truly the Queen's husband though, that would have been something he would have done. He shuddered, her *husband*, the King...

Nathan let out a heavy sigh as he looked once again to the *Firefly.* It's battered and broken frame seemed to yell at him for his stupidity.

Bring me back please, he pleaded hoping to go back to the way things were before this mess. A sharp pain coursed through his back causing him to grimace. Once it faded into the aching he was getting used to however, the thought of leaving no longer appealed to him. He glanced to the castle, he felt an urge to stay, as if he was bound to the city for some unknown reason.

He jumped as he felt a hand on his shoulder. Expecting it to be the Queen he spun around ready to shout at her, accuse her of making the whole thing up, but when he faced the one who approached him it was not the Queen.

"What do you want Armine?" he asked.

"Several of my guards saw you running through the castle. Are you well?" Armine responded.

Nate rolled his eyes, "Like you care."

He heard Armine sigh, "Nathan you are correct in assuming I would rather not have been tasked with you."

"Great pep talk. I feel so much better," Nathan lamented.

"That was before you saved the Queen," Armine stated forcefully. "I was very impressed with *Firefly's* abilities. Despite the fact I thought you were showing off a little at the end. You proved to be a valued asset to our guard." Nate didn't respond to the slight shove he received.

"Showing off?" he asked in disbelief, his trouble with the Queen fading slightly at the prospect of discussing his flying, "You mean when I was spinning in a dive?"

Armine raised an eyebrow, "Of course...it is a ceremonial dive used normally only on great occasion. Though upon further consideration, I suppose saving the Queen would qualify."

"Armine, I stalled," Nate said, "I was in a spin. It happens when...never mind. It wasn't a good thing."

"But you got out," Armine observed.

"Barely. Saving the Queen did a number on the *Firefly's* wings. They could barely support her," Nathan explained. He couldn't imagine how this was so hard for Armine to grasp. The *Firefly's* wings couldn't be that different from his own.

"Regardless..." Armine said softly. Nate rolled his eyes; it was like talking to a wall. "What has you crying in front of your steed?"

Nate frowned, "Trouble with the Queen." When Armine remained silent he continued, "She may have..."

"May have what?" Armine asked. Nate hid his face as a blush spread. Was he really going to tell Armine what happened? It seemed more like a conversation he should have with Nafais, but then that might also be weird considering the Queen had essentially implied that he was now her father.

Next, best thing I suppose, he thought, "She presented her wings to me."

Armine's wings shifted on his back, "Define presented her wings to you," he ordered forcefully.

"She Uhm...laid them out in front of her. On the bed, after I woke up." Nate explain intrigued by Armine's reaction. He expected something of a shock but certainly not this shift from a friend to a military officer.

"Did you accept them? Touch them I mean?" Armine asked again, his tone still equally forceful.

"Uhm...not intentionally."

"Nathan are you aware of the implications of this? The Queen has a King. He may be dead but she is still his and he hers." Armine said, his demeanor slipping back to what it had been before.

Mirage

"Yah...uhm about that," Nate saw Armine's already raised eyebrow raised higher, "She called me her King." There was no immediate response from Armine.

"Tell me exactly what she said."

Nate explained everything, omitting the fact that the attackers were supposedly Armine's family. Armine listened, his face showing no emotion. Finally, he spoke. "I will speak with Nafais. You must return to the Queen and sort this out. If we do in fact have a threat to the city on the loose then we cannot have tension among the royalty."

Nate nodded and Armine took to the sky. Nate looked back to the *Firefly*, sighed and dragged himself towards the castle.

17. The Mirage

The deck pitched as the ship sailed from one cloud to another. Karly grasped a railing to stay upright. She was standing on the upper deck of the *Mirage*. She had been studying it for days and as unlikely as it was, the ship did hold many design traits that her own creations had, even some she had wanted to incorporate into her work but had not been allowed to. She looked to the sails, they glinted in the sunlight. They looked so fragile but when held in one's hands they were stronger than steel. The *Mirage* burst through a cloud sending a spray of moister everywhere. She had given up trying to figure out how a ship she was assured could not fly was able to be supported on clouds.

"Are you enjoying the view?" Shadow asked as he climbed the ornate stairs.

Karly nodded, "Just trying to wrap my head around this whole thing."

Shadow gave her a friendly hug, "Once we return your wings, all will be right. I assure you."

"How does that work?"

Mirage

"My plan was to use the wings of the Queen but my men failed to retrieve her. One of them has kindly agreed to take her place," Shadow explained. With that, a man was dragged in front of Karly. "The sun is in its place, now is the time my dear."

"Please no!" the man shouted, "We had no chance against that thing!"

Karly stared at Shadow, then the crew. She had noticed the fear in their eyes before; they were always trying to please their Captain, and it seemed though that it was more out of their dependence on life than out of respect.

"Shut it featherbrain. There's no such thing as a metal bird," one of the men, Karly assumed to be a guard snapped.

"Metal bird?" Karly asked, "What kind of bird?"

"Iris he is but an unworthy man trying to get out of his commitment," Shadow assured, "Come we must begin."

"What does this entail?" Karly asked.

"You will receive your wings through the sacrifice of another," Shadow explained.

Karly's eyes widened as she realized just what the restrained man was afraid of, "No! You can't just take someone's appendages and staple them onto someone else."

"Where has this come from?" Shadow asked, "You are Iris, Mistress of the Lightning. You never showed compassion as such. You are a Goddess among us and you need your wings to take your throne."

"I am not any goddess! I am a Safety Officer at a race track," Karly argued.

"Very well then. Bring her now," Shadow ordered. Before Karly could react, she felt something bash against her skull.

18. City of the Clouds

Nate quietly walked down the hall towards the Queen's Chambers. His mind was swimming with questions and memories. He reached the chambers only to find them empty. It made sense the Queen was not going to stay put; she had a job to do. He wandered around looking for her till he finally came to Nafais's chambers. He knocked then realized that Armine was supposed to talk with her. He was about to retreat when he heard shouting.

"You have no right Armine!" Nafais shouted, followed by Armine's muffled reply, "So what...he just left us?" Nate felt something tug at him as if drawing him into the room but resisted. He shifted his shoulders as his muscles seemed to become knotted with the pain intensifying. He pushed open the door in time to see Nafais throw a blade that embedded it into the wall.

"Nafais please..." the tip of another blade lifting Armine's bowed chin silenced him. Nate watched in fascination; he hadn't thought Nafais to be so easily angered. This fact though was overshadowed as he felt the knots in his shoulders getting tighter and the pain blooming across his back.

"I should have you executed for leaving me undefended and attempting to mislead me."

"Nafais why would he sacrifice his only way home for nothing! The Queen is not his monarch," Armine argued. Nate stepped into the room to try and calm Nafais but a searing pain shot through his back again preventing him from speaking. His mouth fell open and then he gritted his teeth.

"And as for your transgression against me personally? Do they hold no weight?" Nafais asked, lifting Armine's head higher.

Nate fought through his pain and grasped a wooden staff. He thought he knew that Nafais would never hurt Armine but now he wasn't so sure. Better safe than sorry.

"I hold only one regret Nafais, that I was not good enough to be your mate," Armine replied evenly. Nafais seemed to seethe with anger.

The pain in Nate's back reached a crescendo. He felt something in his back give and intense pain shot through him as Nafais spun around and threw her blade at the wall. Before the blade even hit he saw the surprise in her eyes, then he felt something odd. It was like the parting of hairs only much stronger and something that was completely foreign to him.

"Nathan?" Both Armine and Nafais said in unison.

"I don't believe it," Nafais whispered. Nate followed her stare to see her blade impaled in a wall of blood covered feathers. To his shock it was a wing, and that wing was attached to his own back. He stood speechless as the pain in his back faded, suddenly feeling lightheaded. He flexed his new wings finding them easily manipulated.

"Do you believe me now Princess?" Armine asked.

Nafais slowly nodded, "I don't understand how this is possible. Does the Queen know?"

"I will retrieve her from the throne room," Armine replied, and left.

Duh...of course she would be in the throne room, Nate scolded himself. He then tried to walk forward only to find himself pinned to the wall with the blade. He gave the wing a yank only to be rewarded by a dull pain coursing through his body. He looked to Nafais who only watched him. Nate reached for the blade to pull it out but found it firmly wedged in the wall.

"That's a hell of an arm Nafais," Nate commented.

"Why?" Nafais asked finally, "Why leave? Do you know the pain you caused my mother, your wife?" The bite in Nafais' words was palatable.

Nate held up his hands defensively, "I don't know what you're talking about. This is all new to me."

"New to you? You are the King, my father and you never said anything! Don't even try denying it; you were the only man to have pure white wings in recorded history," Nafais argued.

"Nafais, I'm telling you I'm as surprised as you are, but I am not your father." At that moment, the Queen and Armine arrived.

The Queen stepped to Nate and removed the blade from his wing. She gently caressed the new limb causing Nate to wince. "My King," she whispered. Nate wrenched the wing from her grasp only to knock over many items with the other.

"Would someone please explain what's going on?" he yelled.

Mirage

"How can you not remember your own child?" Nafais asked angrily.

"Daughter. It is not his fault," the Queen reassured. "I fear that the Mistress of Lightning has messed with his memories. It is likely that in order to subdue him and have a chance to escape, she would have to make him belong in that world."

"Mistress of Lightning? You mean the witch's tale of the *Mirage* and Captain Shadow?"

"It is more than a witch's tale I am afraid. Come daughter I will explain." With that, a disgruntled Nafais and Rosa left Armine and Nate alone in the Princess of the Sky's chambers. Nate paid Armine little mind as he flexed his wings, finding them surprisingly easy to manipulate. A cough brought his attention to the black winged guard.

"What?" Nate asked. Armine gestured towards the door. It took a few seconds but Nate realized that he really shouldn't be in Nafais's room without her present. He smiled bashfully, his wings tucking tight to his back as he followed Armine out of the room. He felt the blood on his wings smear on his back. They walked in silence down the hallways before Nate spoke up again. "Would I be able to shower or something?"

Armine let out a short laugh, "I am bringing you to a surgeon. He will clean the blood."

"So what does this mean? Do I have powers like the Queen?"

Armine let out a curt laugh, "The King was not of the same lines as the Queen. He was a common worker who managed to attract the attention of our gracious ruler. Or at least those are the stories. You would know better than me."

"Except I don't," Nate muttered, "What about the Mistress of Lightning?"

"An old tale told to young kids," Armine explained, "It is said that this Mistress lived in the thunder clouds that roam the sky. She was at the time in the employ of the Queen, building a transport vessel that could sail on clouds. However, she was not satisfied with her ship. She wanted to build an attack vessel. To attack what was never known. She allegedly seduced a royal guard and made an attempt on the Queen's life though. Both were sentenced to exile and stripped of their wings but not before vowing destruction of our city."

Nate stopped dead in his tracks, he looked to Armine and pieces began to fall into place. "Rosa is right, there's more to it than a simple *tale.*"

"What do you mean?" Armine asked.

Nate shook his head as memories began to trickle into his mind, "Did they ever tell you what happened to your family?"

Armine arched an eyebrow, "My family are alive and well."

Nate hesitated before responding, "Good." If Rosa had kept what Nate now knew a secret for so long then there was no need to bring it up.

"What do you know?"

"Nothing," Nate lied.

Armine eyed Nate suspiciously, "What of my family?"

"Trust me Armine you don't want to hear it," Nate stated and walked ahead of Armine.

"That is not for you to decide," Armine protested.

"If Rosa wants to keep it secret then I will not betray her," Nate stated feeling a sudden loyalty to his supposed wife.

"Nathan–"

"Do not make me order your mouth shut!" Nate snapped, "For your own good stop pushing."

Nate saw Armine bow his head, "Very well. Come let's get you cleaned up."

19. The Mirage

Karly woke to a flash of light. She was cold, wet, tired and laying on the deck of the *Mirage*. It was dark and pouring rain. Another flash of lightning followed closely by rolling thunder erupted as the deck pitched sideways then settled. Karly slowly rose up looking for any signs of the crew and found them standing off to the side, equally drenched by the rain. As she stood, she felt something pull on her back. She looked back to see a set of gold wings, the same colors as the *Mirage's* sails, attached to her back. She jumped only to slip and fall in a puddle of blood. She gagged as she saw the blood leading to a mangled body that belonged to the sacrificed sailor. She wanted to cry but found a sudden strength as something began to stir inside her, like a part of her subconscious that she never knew existed. Spreading her new wings, she looked to Shadow who wore a huge grin.

"Gentlemen, I present to you Iris, Mistress of Lightning," his commanding voice called. The entire crew fell to their knees.

"Hail!" they all shouted. That stirring inside Karly intensified as she commanded the rain to stop. To her surprise it did, but the lightning, thunder and dark clouds remained. She looked to the *Mirage's* sails, shining brightly in the dark, its white hull seemed to glow as well. She frowned as memories that were not hers flooded her mind.

"Are you alright Iris?" Shadow asked. Karly nodded and took a step to the railings. Her supposed life coming back to her. Building the *Mirage*, the Queen's betrayal, condemning the King. The *Mirage's* purpose and her vow to the Queen and King. Each memory forcing part of her mind away, replacing Karly with Iris.

"I can't believe I did all that," she muttered. She felt a hand on her arm and looked to see the loving gaze of Shadow. Memories of him too came flooding back, forcing out the last of her memories of her life on earth. "You truly loved me."

Shadow smiled, a smile that warmed Karly's altered heart, "I know it must be a lot to take in. You've had a long life; It's time for you to rest."

"Very well. Lead the way," Karly replied.

20. City of the Clouds

Nafais landed on her balcony grumbling to herself, "How could she!" She proceeded to her room and pulled her daggers from the wall. She felt hurt, a dull ache of betrayal from her mother driving her actions.

"He was my father!" she shouted to no one specifically as she threw a blade at the already beaten wall. "I had a right to know!" Another blade was embedded into the wall. "And so does Armine." Nafais marched to her door, flung it open and yelled down the hall at a guard.

"Tell Captain Armine I have important business to discuss with him." Nafais ignored the look she got from the guard and slammed her door shut. She paced around the room flexing her wings as she calmed down. In retrospect, some of her mother's actions made sense. She could have not retrieved the King without the risk of freeing the Mistress of Lightning. How the woman had gained magic and immortality outside of the royal lines was still a mystery to Nafais, but it was there. The Queen would also likely have had an easier time explaining to her daughter and everyone else that the King had died in a flying accident then that he had been trapped while banishing a monster. That alone would cause riots for his salvation.

Nafais sighed and sat heavily on her bed, tears making their way down her cheeks. She had just gotten her father back and what was she doing? Crying like a little girl alone in her room? Did it even matter? Nathan was clearly not the King that had been the father she had never known. Her mother reassured her that with the reclaiming of his wings his memories would return but it seemed hopeless at the moment. Not even the Queen could hide that fact. A gentle knock came at the door.

"Enter," Nafais called.

"You wished to see me, Princess?" Armine asked as he stepped into the room.

Nafais nodded, her anger from before having faded. She wondered if telling Armine that his father was a cold-blooded murder bent on destroying the thing that Armine was trying to protect was a good idea. Probably not.

"How is Nathan?" she asked instead.

"Fine. We cleaned his wings and they look to be very strong and healthy. He might be a little light headed as his current blood supply was less than needed with the new wings but his body should make accommodations."

"Armine will you hold me please?" Armine arched an eyebrow, "Please Armine. I don't know what to think right now but I know I *want* to be held by you." Armine complied with a hesitant stiff wing draped across Nafais. Nafais sighed happily as she snuggled into its downy surface. "Will you be my Prince, Armine?"

Nafais felt Armine shifted, "Nafais–"

"It's not any alteration speaking Armine. It's me and I want you. Whatever the consequences," Nafais persisted.

"I would be honored my Princess," Armine replied. Nafais smiled and the two remained silent in each other's embrace. "Nafais...Nathan said something of my family. Do you know what he may have been referring to?"

Nafais looked at Armine's face and couldn't bring herself to lie, "Your family is not that of your birth lines."

"But...we grew up together."

Nafais nodded and pulled away from Armine's wing, she knew where this was going, "Are you sure you want to know the answers to your inquiries?"

"Yes, Nafais what's this big secret?" Armine asked forcefully.

"You had a brother and a sister, apparently. Your father was a Captain of the Royal Guard. He was...led astray." Nafais proceeded to explain what her mother had told her of Armine's family, how they were murdered, and the attempt on the Queen's life, the exile and much more. Armine slumped slightly.

"...Your father now commands a Cloud Schooner. My mother fears that he may use it to mount an attack on the City of the Clouds." Nafais finished.

Armine looked up at Nafais, "Knowing all you know when you look at my wings. Yet you still want me as a companion?"

"Your father's actions are not those of yourself," Nafais replied.

"When you saw the black wings on the attackers. You did not think I helped them by leaving you alone?"

Mirage

"I would never accuse you of such things!" Nafais snapped, "Your father was an easily manipulated traitor, seduced by charms of another. You are nothing like that!"

"Then that is all I need to know," Armine replied, "I will not hesitate to defend this city, for he is not my father. The *Mirage* will fall and him along with it."

22. City of the Clouds

Nathan walked down the palace stairs toward the marketplace. He had been searching for the Queen all day only to be told that she had been out at the market. It seemed odd to him that she would be shopping, surely there were servants that dealt with that kind of thing. As he entered the marketplace it was clear though that she was not shopping. There was a sort of spell keeping prying eyes of the marketplace from observing her but on this side of the shield, Nathan could see everything. A memory from when they had first met came flooding back, just after the Guard Race she had been standing in that exact same spot. Nathan slowly approached Rosa. Her wings seemed to twitch as she starred at the *Firefly*. Nate had seen that before but he couldn't place it. He felt his own wings draw tight against his back as he continued his approach. Rosa wings suddenly flared out as she seemed to glare at the *Firefly*. Nate instantly placed that action. He had seen it on Nafais when she had been angry with Armine.

"Rosa?" Nate called tentatively. He briefly wondered if it was his smartest move to interrupt an angry Queen but pushed the concern beside as his concern for her welling being over shadowed them.

Mirage

"Nathan?" Rosa said somewhat surprised. She folded her wings back against her back.

"What are you doing?"

Rosa looked back to the *Firefly*, "Forgive me, my King. Years of rule have worn on me. There are times where I simply must be myself...even when myself is not who I want to be."

Nate watched the Queen carefully. It made sense. No one could be expected to be perfect all the time but why was she getting mad at a machine, "And you are trying to scare the *Firefly*?"

Rosa smiled briefly, "You are learning the language of our wings I see. Yes, I suppose I was. I both adore *Firefly* for returning you to me but also despise it for opening the gate between our worlds. I fear that the Mistress of Lightning is not far off."

"You know it's not alive," Nate commented, "Even if it was, it would be dead by now."

Rosa's face grew grim, "I'm sorry Nathan."

There was a long moment of silence before Nate spoke again, "Who is the Mistress of Lightning?"

Rosa cocked her head to the side, "I don't understand."

"She has magic, right?" Nate asked. Rosa nodded. "And only immortals can control magic and only royal bloodlines are immortal. Correct?"

Rosa sighed, "You are as observant as ever. The Mistress of Lightning, her actual name is Iris. She was...is my sister. She did not take my coronation lightly and vowed to overthrow me."

"But she was under your employ when she built the *Mirage* wasn't, she."

Rosa's wings hung limply, "No she was not. The legend was crafted in an attempt to ease the worry and make it less likely to be questioned. I never enjoy lying to my subjects but at times it is necessary."

Another moment of silence followed before Nate spoke, "So we don't stand much of a chance against the *Mirage* do we?"

"Why would you–?"

"You aren't hunting it down," Nate interjected.

Mirage

Rosa's wings lowered completely, resting on the ground, "I'm afraid so. My sister was nothing if not intelligent and thorough. All we have at our disposal are enchanted arrows. They will do little to the *Mirage*. It is made for destroying the city."

Nate chewed on his lower lip. If that was true they were doomed. There had to be a way for them to fight back and stand a chance; good guys always won after all. Then a thought crossed his mind. Were they the good guys? There was so much that Rosa had kept from him; was there something she had done that warranted her destruction? He looked around the city. It seemed to be perfect and peaceful, and Nafais and Armine were good souls. He looked back to the Queen. He realized it didn't matter what the Queen had done. No innocent person deserved to die because of it. It was then that a glint of sun off the *Firefly* caught his eye.

"Enchanted arrows you say?"

23. The Mirage

The deck of the *Mirage* was abuzz with activity as it sailed through the skies. Karly stood on its upper deck at its helm. She finally understood how the vessel was able to support itself on the clouds. She...or rather, Iris, had enchanted the hull with a spell that allowed it to remain airborne but only on clouds. It would sink like a stone in the open air. She flexed her golden wings. Acclimatizing to the new appendages was surprisingly easy and she found the remorse she felt for how she obtained them dwindling. She still didn't trust herself to try flying yet though.

Karly watched Shadow as he called gentle but firm orders to his crew, ensuring the ship sailed as per her direction. She had to admit he was rather attractive and there was a stirring within her when she was near him, or she supposed, inside Iris.

Why? Why did this happen to me? She asked herself. She looked in the direction of their voyage. They were supposedly returning to claim her crown or something like that. Something about a City of the Clouds under an unjust rule during her absence. However, for the life of her Karly could not remember Iris ever being crowned anything. Her memories were still coming back to her, despite her having lost most of the ones from her pervious life on earth.

"You look troubled," Shadow said from behind her.

"I am," Karly replied simply, "What kind of merchant sails a warship?"

Shadow chuckled, "I never said this was a merchant vessel now did I?"

Karly stared at Shadow, "Then..." memories flooded her mind as the real reason for their voyage snapped into place, "I built this ship to destroy the City of the Clouds."

Shadow clicked his tongue, "Not exactly. You built it to reclaim your throne after your sister took it from you."

"Right," Karly responded. She resisted the urge to sigh, the memory of deceiving Shadow burned into her mind, along with her orders for him to kill his family to prove his loyalty. Soon though along with the memories came the resentment toward the Queen. She gripped the railing tighter as more and more memories flooded her mind.

"I see your memories are returning," Shadow remarked.

Karly simply nodded, "It's alright if you would like you can retreat below deck. I can bring the ship into position while you rest."

"No," Karly stated firmly, "If I remember correctly there are many people in that city. I do not wish to simply destroy it."

Shadow seemed perplexed, "What of making the Queen pay by watching her empire fall to you and your ship?"

"Is it really a victory if we destroy our prize?" Karly asked.

Shadow seemed to consider this, "I suppose that makes sense. Why the change in plan?"

Karly considered this. She did want this Queen to pay but she distinctly remembered hating her more before her banishment, "Let's just say my time away has allowed me time to calm down and approach the situation more rationally." There was a moment of silence as Karly contemplated the attack plan. The Queen needed to die, for some reason, but she didn't want to destroy the city. If that was what they were fighting over, it would make no sense.

Mirage

"I believe that a more precise infiltration method is
required."

24. City of the Clouds

"It's ridiculous!"

"Preposterous!"

"Impossible!"

"It could work." All the Mystics looked to their leader, Hexane. The older mystic simply shrugged, "The enchantment may hold on any nonliving object."

"But the power required–," one mystic protested.

"Is within the Queen's abilities."

"Uhm..." Nate tried to interject but was interrupted.

"And what of the *Mirage's* armaments?"

"The enchantment will not provide protection against them but if he can hit the ship it will cause significant damage."

"I have a question," Nate tried again.

"And if the enchantment fails?"

"Then it fails and he will die," Hexane replied. The other mystics shrugged and nodded.

Mirage

"Hey!" Nate yelled. No one paid him any mind. He was getting a little annoyed. Was he not supposed to be their King? Shouldn't they be listening to him?

"What is it, my King?" Rosa finally asked.

Nate let out a sigh of relief. "Even if the enchantment works there's still another problem. The *Firefly* needs fuel in order to fly and her wings need to be repaired. Right now, it is useless magic or no magic."

The mystics murmured to each other for a moment before Hexane addressed the Queen, "My apologies your majesties. We will work out a solution. Till then I must request you leave us be."

"Of course," Rosa's gentle voice replied and she led Nate out into the castle gardens. They walked in silence under the moonlight before Rosa spoke again, "I am sorry Nathan. I have not even arranged a proper welcome for you."

Nate laughed, "It's not the end of the world. You've had other things on your mind. Like the actual end of the world. I have been wondering though, there is no way my name was Nathan."

Rosa laughed softly, "No it is not. You are King Delmar. King of the People." She ran a wing along Nate's back,

"Delmar..." Nathan repeated trying to roll the name of his tongue. He kind of liked the sound of that. "So if I'm Nafais's father then am I supposed to be trying to scare Armine away?" Nate joked.

Queen Rosa let out a very un-lady-like snort before composing herself again. "Forgive me. I do worry about the possibility of a pairing between Armine and Nafais."

Nate looked at his "wife", "Why? They seem like a good match."

"Perhaps," Rosa replied, "But blood is thicker than water."

"Yeah, and water is thicker than oil but that doesn't mean that it can't work."

Rosa stopped in her tracks, "I'm not sure I understand your reasoning."

"Armine is crazy about Nafais. Whether he admits it or not his wings give it away. At least I think they do. He would never betray her," Nate reasoned.

"He left her undefended," Rosa responded.

Nate opened his mouth to reply but found no argument. The attackers were of Armine's kin. He shook his head, "He had nothing to do with that. There's no way that he would do that to Nafais."

"I have worried about him ever since he followed his father's footsteps and joined the guard. But I could not deny his entry."

"He earned his position, right?" Nate asked.

"Yes." Rosa responded quickly, "I would not award unworthy men."

"And his father betrayed you because of love for your sister, right?"

"So it is to be believed."

"Then if his allegiance lies with the one he loves then he isn't a threat as his love is Nafais," Nate reasoned.

"I had not considered that," Rosa replied. She wrapped a wing around Nate. "Perhaps I have been looking for traitors among my people for too long."

Despite his inhibitions, Nate allowed himself a moment to revel in the softness of the Queen's downy wing, his Queen's wing. The sound of someone landing behind them caused the Queen to retract her wing.

"Forgive me my Queen, I did not mean to interrupt," the guard apologized.

Rosa waved it off, "What have you?"

"The *Mirage* was spotted south of the city. Its course will bring it here within a day."

25. City of the Clouds

Armine awoke to a shuffling beside him. He shook the fog of sleep from his mind as he surveyed the room he was in. He went still as he realized the room that was bathed in moonlight around him was not his own. He looked to his side and saw Nafais curled under his wing. A smile graced his lips and he leaned down to give her gentle kiss on the forehead.

"It's too early," the Princess of the Sky groaned in response. Armine chuckled softly as he diverted his attention out the window. He thought of his supposed father, out there sailing. He briefly wondered what it would be like. To sail free and travel beyond the borders of the city. Movement of his love under his wing soon made him conclude it wouldn't be better than this moment. He sighed happily. He was just about to drift back into the realm of sleep when a loud horn sounded through the city. He instinctively shot straight up unintentionally knocking Nafais out of the bed.

"You could have asked me to move," she grumbled as she rubbed her head. Then the horn sounded again and her eyes widen, "The Queen hasn't called the city to battle since...before I was born."

Armine nodded as he quickly dressed in his armor, "I have a feeling the *Mirage* may be close. Quickly Princess get dress."

Nafais burst out laughing, "How can you still call me that after last night."

Armine's forever treacherous wings began to shift on his back. "I have a duty I must attend to Nafais. And so do you."

Nafais smiled and nodded, "You're right. Just promise me something."

"Anything."

"Come back alive."

26. City of the Clouds

Nate and Rosa quickly made their way out to the balcony. Sure enough, off in the distance a thunderstorm loomed. They were both given telescopes and as Nate looked through his, a flash of lightning illuminated the sky giving him the briefest glimpse of the *Mirage*.

"It doesn't look so bad," he remarked. "Looks like a merchant's vessel."

"A merchant vessel with enough magical weaponry to destroy our city three times over," Rosa remarked dryly. "My sister was a little dramatic at times."

"Would they really destroy the city?" Nate asked.

Rosa nodded, "It was her vow."

Hasty footsteps drew the attention of Nate and Rosa, "What going on Mother?"

"The *Mirage* is approaching our borders," Rosa responded. "Captain Armine, prepare a defensive attack. Check with the mystics on the condition of the *Firefly*."

Nate motioned Nafais over. "So...daughter then."

Nafais bowed her head, "So it would seem."

Nate shook his head, "Sorry, it's hard to get my head around, but…" Nate plucked a black feather from Nafais' brightly colored wings. "You may wish to preen before presenting yourself to your mother after taking Armine to bed."

Nafais blushed so hard that her face seemed to glow in the dark, "I…"

Nate silenced her. He looked at her face, seeing so much of the resemblance she had of her mother, and memories he had of Nafais as an infant came rushing back. "I'm sorry I wasn't here to see you grow up."

Nafais laughed briskly. "What? You don't think getting trapped by an evil villain in another world gives you a free pass?"

Nate shook his head.

"My King," Rosa called, "*Firefly* may not be ready but we must be."

Nate nodded. "I'm told you can fight," he said to Nafais. "Protect Armine will you?" Nafais let a small smile slip onto her face as Nate fell into step beside the Queen.

Mirage

"You saw the same feather I did?" Rosa asked.

"We have bigger problems then Armine bedding Nafais. So what's the *Mirage's* weakness?"

"I know of no weakness the ship possesses. My sister is very thorough," Rosa replied as her steps hastened. She waved a guard over.

"It has to have something. Nothing's perfect," Nate protested. There was no response, "Come on, it has to be able to sink!"

"Sink?" Rosa asked.

"You know fill with water. Oh right, it rides on clouds." Nate pondered this thought for a moment before realizing something, "Rosa, what if it's a distraction."

Rosa stopped in her tracks, "Pardon, my King?"

"We know they can sneak into the city undetected. And yet the *Mirage* is certainly putting on a show. What if it's meant to draw our forces to one side of the city while there's attack from the other?" Nate explained. Before either could react through a loud explosion rang out as a shot from the rapidly approaching *Mirage* decimated the top of a building.

"My Queen! Get to the–" the rest of the sentence was lost as another shot from the *Mirage* hit.

The Queen grabbed Nate's hand, "Send word to Captain Armine. He must raise the defenses." With that, she dragged Nate to the upper levels of the castle. They reached it just in time to see a wave of blue light sweep over the city. The next shot from the *Mirage* exploded harmlessly out in front of the city walls.

"Wow," Nate gasped.

"They won't hold forever," Rosa murmured. "The *Mirage* can break them." As if to prove her point the *Mirage* began to assault the shield with vigor. Shot after shot hit the dome in almost the same spot and already cracks could be seen forming. Nate looked out to the *Mirage*. Even shaded in darkness's it's white hull and gold sails glowed. He watched as the dark clouds seemed to lap at its hull like water.

Like water... he thought. If the *Mirage* used clouds like water, then it couldn't sail without them.

"Rosa!" Nate suddenly exclaimed, "You have control over clouds, right? And Nafais has air?" Rosa nodded. "Nafais can stop a *wind-powered* ship in its tracks and you can take the clouds out from underneath the ship."

Rosa shook her head then stopped. She looked at Nate and smiled. She gave him a hug and a kiss on the forehead, "As innovative as always." She then turned to a guard. "Bring me my daughter."

27. The *Mirage*

Karly watched with satisfaction as the *Mirage* continued its assault. The shields wouldn't last forever. She was pleased to see her sister had not changed from her memory. Content to hide behind her magic rather than mount an offensive. That was fine with Karly as Iris's magic had yet to come into play. She closed her eyes and channeled the energy around the *Mirage.* Then a bolt of lightning struck the shield surrounding the *City of the Clouds.* The shield shattered leaving them defenseless once again. Karly stumbled back slightly from the force of magic she'd used. She was caught by a set of black wings that helped her to right herself.

"Wonderfully done my darling," Shadow purred. Karly let a small smile play on her lips. She flexed her wings.

"Now then. Blow their gates."

Shadow nodded, "Hard to port! Arm the side guns!" The *Mirage* wasted no time getting into position and soon a barrage of magic weapons assaulted the gates of the city. Iris looked at the castle, content that the battle was hers. Then the wind changed. The air currents around the *Mirage* swirled as the sails began to luff leaving the *Mirage* without propulsion.

Mirage

"My niece," Karly grumbled. Though Nafais had only been young when Karly had been banished, she still exhibited control over the air. That control was something that Iris would have no hope of fighting. It didn't matter though; the *Mirage* was within striking distance. The Queen of the Clouds would fall tonight. Then something happened that Iris had not considered. The clouds under the stationary *Mirage* dissipated leaving nothing but air. With all the men on one side of the vessel and with its support gone the ship began to roll onto her side before falling into the abyss as arrows pelted the crew.

28. City of the Clouds

Armine watched the *Mirage* as it battered the gates. He looked to the armament of his troops and that of the *Mirage*. It was no competition. The *Mirage* had the bigger guns. He looked at the castle. He could see Nafais and the Queen on the balcony. He had been told they had a plan but if the only thing they could do was steal the wind from the *Mirage's* sails then they were all doomed. Armine turned to his men.

"Archers at the ready!" he called. Hundreds of bows went up. Armine had no doubt in his mind they could win this battle if the Queen took out the *Mirage*. The Queen's army was quite large, the *Mirage's* crew dwarfed in comparison. It was only the *Mirage* that tipped the scales against them. Armine was just about to give the order to fire when the clouds under the *Mirage* vanished. His eyes grew wide as the ship rolled onto its side.

Not wanting to miss their chance he called the order, "Fire!" Hundreds of arrows launched at the crew of the *Mirage* as it fell into the abyss. The *Mirage* didn't fall for long. It hit a second layer of cloud well below the city. The sound of wood cracking filled the air as the ship landed on its side. Somehow it managed to right itself but as soon as it did so one of its main masts fell to the side. Still, without wind, it sat on the cloud layer being assaulted from above.

Despite its fall Armine worried about the ship. It was still within firing range so all the crew would need was to rearrange the cannons to continue their fight. It appeared, that was not their concern as many men took flight from the ship. Bathed in moonlight their black wings were almost lost in the night as they climbed towards the city.

Armine raised his bow and fired, clipping the wing of one of the attackers. What he didn't expect was the assault from behind. An arrow just missed his head as another enemy front descended from above. They had been tricked. Armine's men quickly split themselves between the two attacking fronts but the enemy still made it to land. Armine locked blades with one of the blacked winged men. The fact these men were supposed of his kin meant nothing to him. He felt no remorse for what he was about to do despite their apparent blood ties. He grabbed the man's blade with his own wing and pushed the man over the wall, holding him by only his wing.

"Your father will have your head for this," the man spat.

"He's not my father," Armine replied before slicing the man's wing at the joint and letting him fall over the edge. He was just about to return to the other attackers when a woman with gold wings flew overhead towards the castle.

Another distraction, Armine cursed himself. These guys had a plan and they had fallen for everything so far. Armine took to the skies only to be painfully dragged down by his wing. He was thrown on to the ground. He recovered and ripped his wing form the attacker's grasp, rolling away. Leaping to his feet he brought his sword up and faced his attacker—a tall man in a light blue cloak and pure black wings.

"Hello son."

29. City of the Clouds

Nafais tightened the belt on her waist, her blades stowed in the sheaths attached to it. She looked to her mother who watched as Nate was taken by the mystics to the *Firefly*.

Still can't believe he's my father, she thought to herself. She had always imagined her father as strong, brave, heroic and handsome. Not like the frail being that was Nathan. She supposed it was truly just a stereotype, after all, she had only been an infant when he vanished, but still, she had no idea what her mother saw in him. Except maybe his wings.

"I am sorry for my deceit all these years," the Queen said to her daughter as the attack raged on.

Nafais shook her head, "You should be. But now is not the time."

The Queen nodded and only then did she notice what Nafais was doing, "You intend to fight?"

"I'm not letting our people fight on their own. If they are fighting, I am fighting," Nafais responded. Her mother had the illusion that the nobles were above "petty" engagement such as this.

Instead of the argument Nafais was expecting she got only a mere observation from the Queen, "So much like your father." There was a long moment of silence before the Queen spoke again, "Armine taught you how to wield a blade?"

"Yes, he did. Probably saved my life," Nafais responded.

"Be careful of Armine. I trust your judgment Nafais, but I cannot deny my worry over his blood."

Nafais sighed, "His blood ties have no impact on his actions."

"Would you kill Nathan?" the Queen asked suddenly.

"What?"

"Would you kill Nathan? King Delmar? Your father?" the Queen asked again.

"No. Why would you think such a thing?" Nafais shot.

"Then we cannot expect Armine to kill his own," the Queen reasoned.

Nafais's jaw dropped. That was exactly what she had been asking of him. Both of them had only just regained their fathers but if Nafais was in Armine's shoes she doubted she would be able to kill Nathan. Her shoulders dropped; how could she ask that of him?

She would have dwelled on it further if not of the shouting on the other side of the chamber's doors. A crack of thunder erupted and the doors burst open. Nafais drew her weapon. Beyond the woman standing in the door, the guards posted by the door lay unmoving.

"Ah sister! It's been too long," a woman dressed in a shimmering black dress with gold wings exclaimed joyously as she walked in as if she owned the place.

Sister? Nafais asked herself. Revelations such as this should have surprised her but it was far too normal an occurrence now. *So she is royal blood. What else is mother keeping from me?*

"Iris," the queen responded, her voice cold as ice.

"Is that any way to treat your long-lost sister?" Iris asked, "Although you were always a peculiar one."

The Mistress of Lightning gracefully walked over to Nafais. "My dear niece how you've grown." Nafais stopped her supposed

Aunt in her steps by placing a blade to the woman's throat. "You trained your own daughter to defend you? Tsk Tsk, Rosaria."

"Says the woman who hides behind the *Mirage*," Nafais growled.

"Nafais learned of her own volition," the Queen remarked.

Iris seemed to consider this for a moment before she smiled, "Let's see how she fairs against true power." With that thunder cracked again and lightning hit Nafais' blade.

30. City of the Clouds

Armine glared at the man that was supposed to be his father. He had anticipated some form of sympathy or something that would discourage him from killing the man that had helped bring him into this world, but the knowledge of what his father had done and what he could still do to Nafais prevented such thoughts. He spun his blade and slashed towards his father. The man sidestepped the attack, blocking it with his own weapon.

"What, no hello?" Armine's father observed.

"I do not welcome Captain Shadow into my city," Armine growled and swung again. This time he was quick enough grazing the man's outer wing. Although shallow, it would surely be painful. His success was nothing in the grand scheme of things as a blade carved a gash in his arm. Armine could feel blood trickle down his arm as he stared his father down.

"Let me guess? Captain Armine right? Captain of the Royal Guard? Defender of the Princess and Queen? Just like your old man." Shadow's voice seemed to almost mock Armine as if it proved that he was the same man only younger.

"My father works as a librarian at the archives," Armine snapped. Another cut to the leg brought forth more blood from Armine's body.

"Yet it's my blood that runs from your wounds and my wings on your back," Shadow observed evenly. "They will betray you; the White Guard will be the undoing of the city and you will be tossed aside like a used towel."

White Guard? Armine asked himself.

Shadow turned around, to do what, Armine would never know. He saw his chance and took it. He slashed the man's leg. Shadow winced and spun around only to be greeted with a punch to the jaw. Armine fought through his pain and twirled his blade.

"You may be top of the line on the *Mirage* but your crew is nothing against my men," Armine stated and grabbed his slightly dazed father by the wing. They swung around till both plummeted off the wall of the city. Armine quickly recovered executing a sharp turn before circling back to go after his father once again. They locked blades as they flew.

Mirage

"You think less of me for my actions, but what is a man that will murder his own father?" Shadow asked. Armine faltered. He had faulted this man for murdering his bloodline but yet here Armine was doing the same thing. It was the first remorse he had felt the entire battle and this hesitation was all that Shadow had been waiting for. A blade sliced into Armine's wing.

31. City of the Clouds

Nafais shook her head as she raised herself from the floor. The lightning blast had hit hard, all but obliterating her sword. It had miraculously missed her, singeing her body and sending her flying into the wall rather than killing her. The hit against the wall had hurt her back and wings and also blurred her vision. As her world came back into focus, she saw Iris approaching her mother. Without hesitation, she shifted the winds and forced the woman back. She placed herself between Iris and the Queen, her remaining blade at the ready. Adrenaline drove her through the pain of her injuries.

"You are quite the resilient one," Iris remarked as she drew her own weapon. Nafais responded by lunging. Her blade grabbed the women robe slicing it down the side, but missing the body underneath.

"I must admit you have beautiful wings. A shame they will have to be wasted," Iris mocked. Nafais was about to lunge again but stopped. Iris wasn't engaging with her. She was only defending herself from Nafais. She eyed her supposed aunt suspiciously.

"What is it you truly want?" Nafais asked.

Mirage

Iris looked at the queen, "Why have you not told her, sister? How you ripped the crown from my head?" Nafais swung her blade cutting off one of Iris's wing tips.

"You will not address the Queen in such a manor."

Iris, clearly biting through the pain of her injured wing, looked to Nafais, "You would really defend her without justification?"

"No," Nafais replied. "I defend her because she needs no justification." She swung her blade again, this time it was met with Iris's weapon.

"She stands by as you fight her battle. What kind of mother doesn't defend their child?" Nafais ignored Iris's dig at her mother. Truth be told she was a little vexed by her mother just standing there but that was not going to change anything.

"My defense would only be a hindrance to my daughter," the Queen remarked as Nafais' blade swung again and found a target, slashing Iris's face. Unfortunately, Iris's blade also found Nafais, slashing her abdomen. The cut was not fatally deep but deep none the less and seeped blood, staining her clothing. Then her body erupted into pain and Nafais fell. She tried to stand, but every movement resulted in a fresh shot of pain into her system. It felt as though electricity were burning through her body.

Iris chuckled as she raised her glowing blade. Nafais lowered her head, ready to accept her fate. She was injured and now, dark magic was rendering her useless. She had lost. There was a loud crash followed by a shrill cry of surprise. Nafais pain vanished and as she raised her head, she saw a flash of white and gold as two beings rolled across the floor. Nathan came out on top. His short dagger at the ready. He didn't, however, kill Iris. He hesitated and, in that time, she turned the tables. Pinning him down she raised her own weapon only to stop as an elegant hand plunged an emerald green sword through her back.

Nafais looked to her mother in surprise. Iris seemed to be immobilized with the bade in her back. She began to cough up blood onto Nathan's pure white wings.

"Nathan!" Nafais called, wincing in pain, "End her!" Nathan's eyes went wide but he didn't comply. Before Nafais could move the Queen withdrew her blade and bashed the hilt against the woman's skull. She then shoved Iris off Nathan leaving the dying woman to lay spasming on the ground. The Queen fell to her knees by her King. Nafais forced herself to stand and approached the two, the shocks of electricity now completely gone. There was the charge of unreleased lightning in the air.

Nafais approached the dying Iris, "You...you don't know...what...she has...done," Iris said between coughs of blood.

"Oh shut up," Nafais replied and quickly slit the woman's throat. Her lifeless body fell to the ground in a heap. Nafais looked to her mother and Nathan. They were locked in a gentle kiss. Nathan's white wings stained red from Iris's blood. She felt her own blood-soaked clothing beginning to stick to her body. She coughed as loud as she was able to, causing her parents to disengage from their kiss. They both looked away from Nafais.

"Sorry," Nathan mumbled.

Nafais shook her head, "You just saved my life. You don't have to be sorry." Nafais carefully extended her wings. They ached from her hit against the wall but nothing seemed broken.

"Let me tend to you," her mother insisted. Nafais graciously accepted. Her clothes were parted and her mother's face seemed to fall, "My word Nafais." Nafais looked to see what had startled her mother, knowing it couldn't be anything good. Her skin on one side of her body had been blackened like burnt coal. She hadn't had time to assess what the lighting had done to her, but as she examined her arm that held the blade that had been struck, she saw that it too was burned black, and blue lines from her burnt nerves ran all across the rest of her body. It held no pain, however. Only one thought concerned her at that moment.

Armine will never look at me the same way. She let out a heavy sigh. Then something else occurred to her. Armine was still out fighting.

"Nathan get me a cloak," she ordered. Nathan raised an eyebrow but left to find one. The Queen continued to dress her daughter's wounds in the meantime.

"You should not order your father as such," she commented.

"I need to get out there," Nafais replied, "Armine may still need my help."

"Armine is a very capable fighter," the Queen pointed out, "Why a cloak?"

Nafais hesitated, she didn't want her mother knowing of her petty reasons for the cloak, "Easy to find," she replied simply. The Queen didn't seem to buy it but didn't protest either. Nathan returned moments later with a green cloak in hand. Nafais took it, and making sure to cover her scars with it, she set out to find Armine.

32. The Mirage

Armine struggled with his wing but it was no use. His father had missed the bone but had carved out a large number of his feathers rendering the wing basically useless. Resigning himself to his fate Armine folded his wings and directed his dive towards the *Mirage*. He crashed through one of her sails breaking most of his fall. Even so, he hit the deck with painful speed. He rolled, feeling the bone of one of his wings break.

He groaned as he rose to his feet, and looked around. The ship was deserted, evidently deemed a lost asset to the battle. Furthermore, his father had not followed Armine's fall, likely thinking, he was doomed to fall forever. He looked around the battleship and then extended his wing for examination. He winced as his one fully feathered limb refused to move. They were both useless until they healed. That would be painful and irritating for sure. He cautiously walked towards the *Mirage's* helm, gingerly holding his broken wing against his back. If he was stuck here, he might as well see if he could use the *Mirage* to his advantage. Much to his dismay, it appeared that the ship needed at least five crew members to sail her.

Mirage

"Great. Just great," he mumbled to himself. He looked at the clouds surrounding the ship and sighed. It was pointless, even if he did manage to sail it they would get nowhere. The cloud layer wouldn't allow it. The wind rustled his feathers and he looked to the city. If Nafais had allowed the wind to pick up then she must be in trouble.

*I have to help...*he told himself. He would need the Queen's help and some men. He was about to go below deck when something caught his attention. A drop of something landed on his foot. He looked up at the sails. A dark liquid seeped from them, shining in the moonlight. It was almost like the sails were bleeding. Then he realized it wasn't only the sails. The white railings on the *Mirage* were turning red. Then the winds began to blow stronger and the ship rocked on the clouds. The wood groaned as the golden sails shattered into millions of pieces. Armine watched in fascination as shards of golden sails flew around the ship.

Not shards, he realized, *birds,* hundreds of golden birds circled the *Mirage* as it continued to rock on the cloud layer. Armine's own now useless wings began to flutter as he realized what this could mean. The *Mirage* was sinking, and he was

trapped on board.

33. City of the Clouds

Nafais soared over the battle. She should have been down there with the men but she had to find Armine. She had searched almost the entire city for him, letting her hold on the winds drop as she did so. She had failed to find him though. With a sigh she looked down the abyss, fearing he may have made the ultimate sacrifice. That's when movement caught her eyes. She focused her vision on where she saw the movement and was left speechless as she watched the *Mirage*'s sails shatter. The ship began to rock back and forth as the shattered sails spun like a tornado around the beaten vessel. The sound of cracking wood, far louder than it should have been filled the air and managed to stop the battle as every man watched the *Mirage* die. Its hull blew outwards and it rolled onto its side. Nafais felt her heart leap as she realized the city's greatest threat was no more. Her relief was short lived though as she heard a blade swinging. She moved but not quickly enough. The blade hit her leg adding to her wounds. She drew her own weapon and spun around, lashing out with her bad wing catching the assailant in the jaw with the tip. She winced in pain and lost the last of her control of the winds. They swirled violently around disrupting the clouds as the *Mirage* continued to die. Nafais wasted no time. She threw her blade at her attacker. The man dove but a quick change in the air column drove it right into his back. Tucking her wings against herself she dove after the dead body and retrieved her dagger.

"Princess of the Sky!" a guard called, "Captain Armine was seen falling towards the *Mirage*." Nafais felt her heart seize in her chest.

"You are certain he is onboard?" she asked evenly.

"Yes, my Princess. He was wounded by the *Mirage's* Captain," the guard explained. Nafais looked in time to see the last of the *Mirage's* bow slip below the clouds. Nafais clenched her fists tight around her blade.

"Captain Shadow still lives?" Nafais asked, her tone dark.

"Yes, my Princess."

"Not for long." The winds increased in ferocity, howling by as Nafais dove towards the battle. Two hands pulled her from her dive before she could reach the action. "Let me go!" she cried.

"You are in no condition to fight, daughter," the Queen replied evenly. Nafais looked to see the Queen and Nathan holding her. Nathan seemed to be having difficulty maintaining his flight but held her injured body none the less.

"Armine is not going to be too happy if I let you die, now is he?" Nathan joked; the exertion clear on his face.

"Armine's dead!" Nafais shot.

"Are you sure?" the Queen asked.

"He was on the *Mirage*!" Nafais yelled, "It fell in battle."

"Yet it sails towards the city," the Queen observed. Nafais wrenched herself from her parent's grasp to look in the direction the Queen was referring to. The clouds to the east of the city swirled as the winds shifted and then a ship bearing silver sails and a sky-blue hull burst from the dark cloud bank.

"I thought...there...there was only one cloud...schooner?" Nathan panted.

"There is," the Queen responded, "She is named the *Mirage* as it reflects the inner soul of its Captain." Nafais watched as the ship sailed towards the city. It cut gracefully through the clouds before its sail retracted and, what must have been an entirely new crew, leaped from it's deck. Their silver wings glittered in what little light there was left from the shaded moon.

"It went down..." Nafais mumbled.

"And claimed a new Captain," the Queen finished, "Yet it appears that our good Captain has more to him than black wings." The *Mirage's* new crew launched into battle against Captain Shadow's crew, black against silver, light against darkness. Nafais looked at the *Mirage.* She could see Armine standing by her helm. A smile spread across her face just before Nathan's strength failed. The King's wings buckled.

34. The Mirage

Armine threw the wheel of the *Mirage's* helm to the left causing the ship to broadside towards the city. As previously ordered, the crew stowed the sails to prevent them getting too close to the city. His new men wasted no time at all. He needed not to give them orders for they knew. They were to eliminate his father's crew.

He looked towards the city to see Nafais, the Queen, and Nathan watching the *Mirage*. He thought he was dead when the *Mirage's* hull gave out but it made sense now. This Mistress of the Lightning may have built the *Mirage* but the spell she used to allow it to sail tied her to it. Meaning when she died, it too died. But because of the nature of the spell, it could survive if it had another soul to take the place of the Mistress of Lightning. In this case, Armine had been in the right place at the right time. The spell gave the *Mirage* new life and a new crew. Giving the City of the Clouds the upper hand.

"Run out the guns," he ordered. The few men that remained rushed below decks. Armine knew the weapons would be useless against the men who approached the *Mirage* but looking intimidating was always a good deterrent. He looked back to

Nafais just as Nathan began to fall. He was about to take to the skies, spreading his newly healed wings when he heard someone land behind him.

"Taking my ship are you boy?" his father growled behind him. Armine drew his weapon, his wings tingling with a dull pain as if to remind him what this man had done.

"Someone took my flight. I had to improvise," Armine replied.

He could hear his father smirking, "You really think you can beat Captain Shadow? Commander of the only Cloud Schooner in history? Right hand to the most powerful goddess to ever live?"

Armine's good wing shot out knocking Shadow down. Armine swung his blade down missing his father as the man rolled away but not the man's wings. His blade sliced Shadow's left wing on the tip, his blade leaving a silver smear on his feathers. Shadow chuckled.

"You really think I betrayed this city? They betrayed me, boy! Have you ever questioned your leader?" Shadow asked.

Mirage

"I have never had the need," Armine responded. He swung his blade again, only to be blocked by Shadow's.

"I've seen that loyalty before. You love her don't you?" Armine didn't respond, he simply pressed the engagement without success, "You know she has taken a King. Or maybe it's not the Queen who has your eye? Perhaps her daughter? I bet–" Shadow was cut off as Armine's blade finally hit its mark leaving a large gash in the man's leg. Shadow fell. Armine's blade raised his chin. They remained silent for a heartbeat before Shadow growled again, "Go on! Do it!"

"I will not kill you," Armine replied. "Men!" He wasn't entirely sure what to call the men but he somehow trusted them none the less. "Restrain this waste of flesh."

"Yes Captain," one of the sailors answer and they quickly moved to do as ordered.

"I hardly think that's necessary Captain Armine," the Queen's voice said from behind Armine. Armine turned and fell to his knees. When he looked up he saw an exhausted Nathan clutching the *Mirage*'s railing, and the Queen. He did not see the one he wanted to see. Nafais was gone.

"Weakling," Shadow grumbled.

The Queen's gaze fixed on Shadow, "How does it feel Shadow? To have your own ship abandon you?"

"My Queen will have your head for this," Shadow spat.

A loud thud sounded as a body was dropped on the deck. Nafais made a clumsy landing in front of it, "I highly doubt that."

"Iris?" Shadow asked. "How dare you! I will gut you...you...you despicable piece of–"

The Queen slapped Shadow across the face. Armine, Nafais, and Nathan all stared at her in shock, "You do not speak to my daughter in such a manner!" Shadow seemed wise enough to hold his tongue. "Your men have been defeated, your ship lost, your leader killed. You will be tried for your actions and sentenced. Till then I bid you not speak another word."

The Queen then turned towards Armine. "I trust I will no longer have to fear the *Mirage?*"

Armine looked to Nafais who smiled weakly just before Nathan burst out laughing. All eyes turned to him, "What? He even looks for her approval not to be a traitor."

Mirage

35. City of the Clouds

Nate looked over the City of the Clouds from one of the castle balconies. The sun had just begun to rise and repairs would soon be underway. The battle may not have been as bad as it could have been but it left its scars. He was never going to be able to un-see Nafais' burned and beaten body. Never be able to understand how she continued to fight and also never get his wings truly clean of blood; the blood of the one he once called a sister. He shook his head, the images of her mutilated body haunted him despite the memories of Karly slipping away daily. Rosa had assured him the wound would heal with time but for now it was still fresh.

He sighed as he looked to the makeshift dock. The *Mirage* sat peacefully on a bed of clouds. Her sails rolled tight, its new Captain was almost surely with Nafais at the moment. For some reason, it made his skin crawl. There was nothing wrong with Armine of course. He seemed a very suitable partner for Nafais but there was something that was nagging at him. Captain Shadow had lost all his feathers since his engagement with Armine. Something about a magic coating on Armine's blade. He would likely also lose his leg. Nate stretched his wings. He was getting more used to them the longer he was in the city. His role as King though was a little harder to adjust to.

He was pulled from his thoughts as the Queen's wings wrapped around him and she rested her head on his shoulder, "Good morning, my King." Nate smiled, he could feel his affection for the Queen growing every day and rather enjoyed their time alone.

"Good morning," Nate replied as he continued to survey the city. He grimaced as he looked to the beat-up *Firefly*. The last reminder of what his old life had once been.

The Queen took notice. "Is it to be my understanding that my mystics could not heal your machine?" Nate nodded. "Does it really matter? You have your wings now."

"I suppose it's just a letting go thing. I'm still trying to adjust to the fact I've been living a lie."

Rosa turned him around and looked into his eyes, "You did not live a lie. You lived another life. Take all the time you need to adjust my sweet. I am just glad to hold you in my wings again."

They remained silent for a few moments till a servant called them for breakfast, "What else is bothering you?"

Nate hesitated. He wasn't really sure if he should say what's on his mind. It had been bugging him ever since they imprisoned Shadow, "What are the implications of Armine commanding the *Mirage?*"

"I don't know what you mean my dear?" Rosa responded.

"You're immortal. Nafais is immortal. Iris was immortal. If Armine commands the magic in the *Mirage* does that make him immortal?"

Rosa pondered his question for a few moments before retracting her wings, "I know not the answer. It is possible my sister's magic has altered him, but unlikely. The blood of an immortal must be given not taken. Even then the procedures is...less then enjoyable."

"So it's been done?" Nate asked. The more history he learned of this place the more fascinated he became.

"Only one individual has every survived the procedure," Rosa explained, "You."

Mirage

Nate stared at Rosa. "I'm immortal?" Rosa nodded. Nate gripped the railing tighter as the implication of his immortality fell on him. "Guess I'm stuck with you forever." At the hurt expression from the Queen he laughed and wrapped his wings around her, "There are worst things in the world."

Rosa smiled, "I'm glad. Now let us get ready. We have a banquet tomorrow to plan for."

36. City of the Clouds

Nafais soared through the cool night air over the City of the Clouds. She usually loved night flying, the way the city lights would flood into the night sky, the way the stars and moon would shine on the cloud layers surrounding the city, making it appear as though the clouds were made of tarnished silver. Now, though, she was plagued with worry and uncertainty. Images of the battle assaulted her mind, the lighting striking her blade, her mother plunging her blade into her sister, Nathan, her own father, covered in the blood of another, and most vividly, the *Mirage* slipping below the clouds with Armine onboard. She felt a tear leak from her eye. It froze to her face in the cool night air.

As she circled around the city she was greeted by the sight of the *Mirage* sitting in its makeshift cloud dock, sails stowed, hull glowing in the dark. She slowed herself into a hover, pondering the vessel. There were so many questions she had that could not be answered about the *Mirage*, and that worried her. She looked to her tower, debating if it was time to return to her chambers, before slipping into a descent towards the *Mirage*. She landed on one of the ship's masts. She felt a familiar sense of longing like every other time she had come to the *Mirage* in the middle of the night.

Mirage

Even though the ship worried her, it still reminded her of Armine, perhaps because it was supposed to be a reflection of his soul or maybe for some other reason.

She sighed; she hadn't seen Armine since the battle. *Half a moon,* she thought to herself, *you've seen each other almost every day since you became friends and now half a moon without seeing him.* It was no fault of Armine's that they hadn't seen each other, in fact, Armine had been going out of his way making time for her. It was Nafais that was at fault. She had been avoiding him. She was scared of his reaction to her wounds. She already knew she was scarred for life. There was no undoing Iris's damage.

Nafais looked to the deck of the *Mirage* and soon found herself stepping up to its helm. As soon as she touched the deck she felt as if she were wrapped in Armine's wings again. She let out a happy sigh. Even though she knew it was an illusion created by the magic of the *Mirage* it was still a feeling she craved. A cool night wind cut through the feeling, making her shiver, and serving as a brutal reminder of the fact it was all fake. Nafais felt her wings droop, their tips resting on the ship's deck.

"Princess Nafais?" a rough voice asked. Nafais spun around, her wings tucking tight to her back, "Forgive me, Princess. I did not mean to startle you."

"No it is I who should apologize. I arrived uninvited," Nafais replied straightening her cloak.

The sailor smiled in the dark, "Captain Armine has made it clear you are always welcome on your ship."

Nafais raised an eyebrow, "You mean his ship."

The sailor shook his head, "The *Mirage* is to be a servant of the Princess of the Skye. Captain Armine has ensured that."

"Oh," Nafais responded. *Why would it be in my service and not that of my mother?*

"Is something bothering you Princess?" the sailor asked.

So many things, Nafais thought. "No I am fine."

"You look unwell," the sailor remarked.

Nafais sighed. She felt that feeling of being wrapped up in Armine's wings once again and felt herself relax a little. Despite this, however, she still couldn't say what truly worried her. However, she took the opportunity to make other inquiries.

"What are you?" she eventually asked.

The sailor smiled, "We are but magical beings born of the *Mirage*."

"But what does that mean?"

"It means that we are tied to our ship. We need no drink or food, only it's magic to survive and serve. It also means that we are tied to our Captain. Connected in a way that allows us to serve efficiently."

That only raises more questions, Nafais thought drily. "Will it change him?"

"Change Captain Armine?" the sailor asked. Nafais nodded. "Small physical changes yes. He will remain the same being he was before commanding the *Mirage,* however."

Nafais nodded and looked to her castle tower. She let out a sigh. She really wished the feeling of wings around her was real. She remained silent for quite a few moments before the sailor broke the silence.

"Princess, may I speak freely?" Nafais nodded but did not speak. "The Captain is worried for you. He fears for your well being. He truly cares for you."

A tear escaped her eye as Nafais took to the air towards her tower.

37. City of the Clouds

Armine adjusted his wings so he could preen them better. He grimaced at the color. When he took over the *Mirage* his wings had healed surprisingly quickly without pain or irritation, but all his feathers now held a silver outline. From a distance his wings still looked jet black but when the light shone on them, they also appeared to shimmer. To him though, they looked unkempt and dirty despite his best efforts. Armine's thoughts turned to his father. His weapon had left a silver streak along Shadow's wing and like a disease, it grew till his wing turned pure sliver. Then in a gust of wind his feathers disintegrated, leaving him with one injured wing and one that bore no feathers. If what the Queen's mystics thought truly happened, the man would be flightless for the rest of his life.

Armine let out a sigh as his thoughts changed again to Nathan, flightless for years and not knowing it, and then to Nafais. He hadn't seen her since the battle. She had ordered he stay away. It bothered him. He wondered if he had done anything wrong but couldn't figure out what. Then he had been informed she had visited the *Mirage* during the night and spoken with his men. He shook his head and set out towards Nafais' chambers. She would be getting ready for the banquet that welcomed the return of the King and victory of the battle.

He reached her doors and a guard stopped him, "The Princess has asked not to be disturbed."

"Let me past, May," Armine commanded. May shook her head, "Let me pass, May, or I will go through you," he growled. What right did Nafais have to ask him to be her partner and then isolate him? And to use his own people against him.

"Captain, I fear I must insist that you leave the Princess be. I also know you would never hurt one of your own."

Armine's wing shot out knocking the guard to the ground; not hard enough to injure her but enough to get his point across. Armine quickly retracted his wing, shocked at his own actions.

"I apologize. I do not know what came over me." Armine helped May to her feet.

"Man, Captain, your wings are strong," May commented rubbing her side. Armine smile apologetically. "I'm still not supposed to let you pass."

Mirage

"I need to speak with the Princess. It is of significant importance," Armine persisted.

May chewed the side of her cheek, "Can I confide something in you, Captain?" Armine nodded, "I have guarded the Princess most of my career. I have never seen her like this. She seems withdrawn and angry. She usually would greet any guard at her post but now...now she passes without a word."

Armine sighed, "This is why I must speak to her. She likely would have seen things that scared her in the battle."

May nodded, "I'll let you pass but if anyone finds out I'll lose my commission."

Armine let out a short chuckled. "You're worried about that?" May nodded. "I would be the one who pulls your commission."

Armine nodded his thanks and pushed the doors to Nafais's chambers open in time to see a knife thrown across the room and embed itself into the wall. Nafais let out a cry of frustration as she paced around her room, twirling another of her blades.

She always was good with weapons, Armine mused.

Nafais, however, failed to notice him.

"What if he hates me now?" she muttered to herself, "I know that! But what did I do? I am forcing him away!" Armine tried to approach her but stopped, he had seen her like this before. Better to wait for the time to interrupt her inner dialogue.

"That's the problem!" she yelled to her wall, "He will forgive me! He's too forgiving. I should never have pushed him away." Nafais ran a hand through her hair and sighed angrily once again. "He will never love me like this."

Her words stung. How could he not love her? Love was not something that just vanished upon one action. For years she was all his heart had longed for. Before this whole ordeal with Nathan he had been so close and now she thought he didn't love her?

"Nafais," Armine called. Nafais let out a shriek and twirled around, her blade at the ready, wings raised aggressively. *Someone's jumpy.* "It's just me."

"Armine," Nafais whispered, then proceeded to hide behind her wings. "How long have you been standing there? And where's May?"

"Why would you believe that I would think any differently of you now?"

"I..."

"Nothing that could have happened in that battle would–"

"You died Armine!" she yelled. "You died and you came back, only better and I don't know what to think. You have the *Mirage,* a new crew, you could be anywhere, have anything with that ship. I was not so lucky. I still bare the marks of battle. I am...I am no longer worth your time."

Armine reached for her but she pulled away, "How can you say that Nafais. You are worth more to me than this entire city."

Nafais shook her head, "Armine...I was injured...I'm not what you want anymore."

"What are you talking about Nafais?" Armine finally grabbed her arm and pulled her to him. It was then he saw the burns. He looked to her wide eye and rolled her sleeve up to reveal the extent of the damage. "What happened?"

"Iris struck me with lighting...sort of. I know I'm ugly Armine, you don't have to say it. It's not only my arm but my whole body is scarred and they...they won't heal," Nafais responded pulling away, "You deserve better than a beaten warrior."

Armine gently laid a hand on her shoulder, "You really think I love you only for your beauty?" He could see the tears trickling down Nafais' face.

"Was it not what drew you towards me in the first place?"

Armine was about to shake his head but hesitated. He had always thought she was beautiful but that was irrelevant now in the grand scope of things. He couldn't exactly peg what it was he loved about Nafais but he didn't care. He just knew he loved her.

Nafais drew her hand away, "See–" Armine grabbed her with his wings pulling her in close and giving her a kiss.

"Your appearance doesn't matter to me Nafais. I fell in love with the friend I grew up with. The one who found me in the archives one day and invited me, out of the blue, for a flight around the city. The one that was always the royal Princess of the Sky in public but alone, inside the walls of the castle, would challenge me to races through the halls. The woman that was always there when I needed her and the one that felt she could confide in me. The princess that talks to herself when she has a dilemma and insisted I train her to fight so she wouldn't burden the guard. I fell for my best friend Nafais, your beauty is only a bonus, a bonus I still get to enjoy because those marks do not change you the slightest in my eyes," Armine explained locking his eyes with hers. He saw the tears well once again in her eyes before she rested her head on his shoulders and started to sob.

"I was...I was so scared when I lost you Armine," Nafais said between sobs. Armine patted her hair, his wings holding her tightly.

"I know," he whispered, "I know. But I kept my promise, didn't I?"

To Armine's joy he saw a smile grace Nafais' lips, "Yes you did."

Armine placed a kiss on her forehead. "And I intend to keep my next promise. For as long as you'll allow, I will stay by your side. No matter what. The *Mirage* may grant me the ability to explore the skies, but it would be pointless as nowhere could compare to your arms."

"Ok now you getting a little corny," Nafais joked. Her tears had dried on her cheeks.

"It helped though," Armine said smiling.

Nafais rolled her eyes, "You sounded like the stories I wrote in my journal." Nafais gasped and clamped her hands over her mouth as she realized what she had just let slip out.

Armine arched his eyebrow. "You wrote stories? In your journal?"

"Don't you dare Armine," Nafais cautioned, backing out of the embrace and glancing at her desk. Armine wasted no time. He ducked under Nafais' wings and stole the journal sitting on her desk then proceeded to brush his feathers along her abdomen, the one spot where he knew she was ticklish.

"Armine! Give it back!" Nafais said between laughs.

"Come and get it," Armine said with a big grin and he flew out the window. He caught Nafais's laugh as she quickly followed.

Mirage

38. City of the Clouds

Nate lay on the Queen's bed gently stroking her hair. They should have been getting ready for the dinner that was being held later that day but neither he nor Rosa wanted to just yet. Nathan and Rosa had spent the morning lounging around; they had eaten a nice breakfast in the castle grounds and gone for a short flight before returning to their chambers to relax. They had laid in their bed, the Queen's head on Nathan's chest as she helped bring Nathan up to speed on the Kingdom and what he would need to know in order to rule alongside her. Rosa had tried to reassure him that he would be fine but despite this, he still worried about the prospect of ruling a Kingdom, among other things.

"Of course, you can reinstate your guard if you so wish, but I don't see much reason for it at the moment," the Queen said playing with Nate's shirt.

That statement pulled Nate from his musing "We had different guards?"

The Queen nodded, "The guard that still exists today was formally known as the Queen's guard. Your guard was known as the White Guard, after your wings and the armor they wore. They would accompany you on your excursions and races while my guard protected the city. After your disappearance, I assimilated both into one general guard. It..." Queen trailed off, "...made things easier."

"Easier? Wouldn't that be more of a headache?" Nathan asked.

The Queen looked away, "Logistically speaking you are right, my King. It was difficult but I managed with little disruption to duty."

Nate tilted his head; he knew the quirk somehow. His memory told him that Rosa always turned her gaze away like that when she was embarrassed. It was one of her only tells when she was wearing her royal façade.

Nathan nodded, "And what about you?"

Rosa looked back to Nate, "I don't understand what you mean, my King."

"I can't imagine my banishment was easy on you Rosa—"

"You needn't concern yourself with my struggles of the past, my King. You are here now. That's all that matters."

Nate rolled his eyes, "Your well-being matters Rosa."

The Queen smiled. "You always used to say that," she whispered, "You were the only one who ever did."

"Well it's true," Nathan replied tilting Rosa's chin up so she could look at him, "Don't ever forget that." For a long moment, Nathan and the Queen stared into each other's eyes before Rosa finally nodded her agreement. Nathan smiled and leaned in giving his Queen a kiss. The Queen eagerly returned the kiss and Nathan let himself get lost in the moment. It felt right, no hesitation, no confusion, just a sense of being complete with his wife. The moment was ruined though as Nate's wing reflected his delight at the kiss. They extended to their full span knocking over a lamp.

Rosa chuckled and caught the lamp after breaking the kiss, "I see you still need some practice with your wings my King."

Nate smiled sheepishly, "Yeah well—" at that moment something heavy careened through the open window and crashed into Nate's side. He was thrown from the bed onto the floor and crushed underneath whatever hit him. As he tried to get his bearings he felt a hand grab him and throw him across the room.

Mirage

The sound of metal clashing as blades collided filled the room as Nate finally recovered enough to see what was going on. What he saw made his jaw drop. In front of him was the Queen, her wings spread aggressively and her blade locked with that of Armine who stood protectively over Nafais. At that moment everyone in the room seemed to realize who their assailant was and both the Queen and Armine's wings lowered as they breathed a sigh of relieve.

"I advise you to at least knock prior to entering my chambers Captain Armine," the Queen cautioned, a deadly edge in her voice.

Armine quickly fell into a bow, "Forgive me, my Queen, my flight path was not what I had intended."

Nate looked past Armine to see Nafais rolling her eyes, "You tackled him out of the sky didn't you Nafais."

Nafais froze and locked eyes with her father, "Uhm..." Nate kept staring before Nafais's eyes fell, "I got the tower's mixed up. This was to be my chambers, not yours."

A small giggle escaped the Queen's lips, "There are easier ways to bed a mate daughter." All three individuals stared at the Queen with slack jaws. "Would you not agree Captain?"

Nate was the first to recover, "I figured the professionalism was just an act but, damn Rosa."

39. City of the Clouds

The main hall of the castle was decorated in joyous colors as the city prepared to welcome their new King. Armine inspected the area as people filed in. There was an excited nip in the air which heightened the excitement. It seemed even that the castle itself was prepared to welcome Nathan's return as King.

Delmar, Armine scolded himself, King *Delmar.* No matter how hard Armine tried he couldn't get himself to accept the new name. Nathan was...well, Nathan. A stranger that needed to learn their ways, not a King. His presence proposed a new problem as well. After the engagement with Shadow and the Mistress of Lightning, Armine had done some looking into the *White Guard* Shadow had mentioned. What he found was upsetting, to say the least. Armine was used to giving orders to the guard not taking them, so he worried that the King would re-instate the White Guard and disrupt his control over the protection of the city.

Armine stopped himself in his tracks, *Control over the city's protection? Since when has that been a concern?* he asked himself. He had never been protective of his position. Then again, his position had never been in danger. He sighed heavily as he walked to greet the King and Queen. He found them in the gardens. He bowed to his majesties upon announcing himself.

"Rise," the Queen instructed. "I trust all is in order?"

"Of course, my Queen," Armine replied. "The Royal Guard has everything under control."

"And the *Mirage's* crew?" Nathan asked.

"Safely on board and ready to defend the city at a moment notice," Armine explained.

Nathan nodded, "Can I have a word with you Armine. In Private?"

"Of course, my King."

"I will see you at the ceremony," the Queen stated respectfully and left. Armine and Nathan watched her leave before Nathan spoke.

"Don't call me King."

Armine's head snapped around to look at Nathan quizzically.

"What do you mean?"

Mirage

"This whole thing freaks me out. I much rather you and Nafais call me by Nathan for now. In private at least," Nathan explained.

Armine nodded, "I understand. I can imagine this must not be easy to adjust to."

Nathan seemed to ponder this for a few moments before speaking again, "And you? How are you adjusting to your command of the *Mirage?*"

Armine stood proudly, "I'm handling the responsibly adequately."

Nathan smiled, "I figured." There was a tense silence before Nathan spoke again, "You needn't worry Armine."

Armine shifted, arching an eyebrow, "I beg your pardon?"

"I'm not going to be creating a new White Guard. Not yet at least. Even if I did you would become the Minister of Arms. You will still have complete control over the defense of the city."

Armine felt himself relax, "I am honored, my King." Nathan tensed. Then Armine realized the possible implications of the King's words. Did Nathan now view Armine as a power-crazed commander that couldn't take orders well?

"Good. Now I must find the Queen again. She certainly manages to wander far in these halls." Nathan turned to leave only to stop, "And Armine, take good care of my daughter." With that Nathan left. Armine stared at the space where he stood. He shook his head and flexed his wings. It was amazing how much Nathan had changed since arriving. Maybe he truly was a King after all.

40. City of the Clouds

Shadow raised his blade to his wife's throat. Tears ran down her face as she protected her children from him.

"Think of what you are doing!" she yelled. Despite her bravado, Shadow could see the fear in her eyes. He smiled, it was time this woman paid for her anger, paid for all the times she had hit him. He was the Captain of the Queen's Guard and she had made him afraid in his own dwelling. He twisted his blade making a cut in the woman's throat.

"Daddy no!" his daughter shouted. Shadow glared at his child, always the supporter of her mother, just like the rest of them. Shadow hesitate no longer and decapitated his wife right before his children's eyes. They cried out in shock and tried to run but he was faster. He looked around the room once the deed had been done. He was covered in blood. The bodies of his traitorous family lay in heaps on the ground with red blood pooled around them. His youngest son, Armine, cried. The boy had never had the chance to grow and be the evil that his mother and siblings were. He was innocent, yet to make any mistakes. But he could. Shadow was to leave no one alive. He raised his dagger ready to take the last life of

his bloodline but his own when a loud knocking sounded at the door.

"Captain Frame! Captain open up. We heard screaming from the streets." The door to his home broke open and he turned only to feel a hand grab him. He turned back to find his son once again, only instead of being an innocent infant he found himself looking at Captain Armine of the Royal Guard plunging a dagger into his heart.

Shadow woke with a start. He was lying on a hard-cold floor. The sunlight bled through the bars of his window illuminating the dust in the air. Shadow paid none of this any mind, fixating on the celling of his cell. He had been betrayed. After all he had done to secure victory, he had lost. His Queen, Iris killed, his men murdered, his own ship taken from his control. He had been stripped of everything and now remained a shell of what was once Captain Shadow. As he watched the ceiling, images of his dream gripped him. They had been completely accurate except for the end. It mattered not though. He would be sent to the gallows and executed on many charges he was sure. The Queen would see to that.

Mirage

If the Queen didn't take his life then his son's poison would surely do it instead. He had already lost the feathers on one wing and it was beginning to go numb now. His leg had begun to turn and would surely shatter like his feathers had. He was done, defeated, and useless.

He closed his eyes as images of Iris's body flooded his mind. She too had been mutilated, murdered when all she wanted was what was rightfully hers. Despite this he felt less remorse then he would have imagined. Realization began to sink in slowly. She had used him. A tool for her purpose and goals. Something that could be disposed of just like now. She had left him and his men to fend for themselves without her magic as protection against the Royal Guard while she settled her own personal score. He had killed his family for her and she had left him to the slaughter.

41. City of the Clouds

Nate shook what must have been the thousandth hand before he and the Queen retreated from the festivities. Once he reached the royal chambers Nate unceremoniously plunked himself on the bed, letting his wings drape haphazardly over the sides.

"How? How can you do that all day?" he asked Rosa.

Rosa's laugh brought a smile to his face, "I know not the answer myself at times."

"Are they always such kiss ups?" Nate asked as he sat up rolling his neck.

Rosa smiled at her King, "The Nobles are the highest class of society. They are also the most peculiar group of individuals. When they wish for your grace they are as you say "kiss-ups" but, alas, once you have done something that they dislike, they are like monsters."

Nathan sat up and stretched his shoulders and retracted his wings to his back. He looked out the window at the city lights. Wisps of clouds painted by the city's glow hung in the sky. Even in the dark, the *Mirage*, in its port, seemed to shine. *Our port, my city.*

Mirage

Nathan thought to himself. *What the hell am I doing? I'm not a King. I can barely lead a dog down the street.* Nathan was too caught up in his inner monologue to notice the Queen taking a seat beside him. *I'm going to be dumping all the responsibilities on Rosa because if I do it, it will only end horribly, and that's unfair. I'm supposed to be this King of the people but when was the last time I looked out for someone other than myself and my sister?*

"What troubles you, my King?" Rosa asked.

Nathan shook his head, "Nothing," he muttered.

Rosa was quiet for a while before she spoke again, "You are worried you won't be the King we all want?"

Nathan looked at her, "How did you–?"

"You had the same concern when you took my hand in marriage. You need not worry. Being yourself will be all you need to lead. You already have the respect of many for just the actions during the battle alone."

Nathan nodded; it would be fine. He laid down on the bed and sighed happily as he felt the Queen's wings drape over him.

They were so soft that he quickly felt sleep taking him. Just before he drifted off, he heard the Queen speak softly.

"Goodnight, my love."

"Goodnight, my Queen," he murmured and slipped into the land of dreams.

42. City of the Clouds

The sound of a metal door grinding open pulled Shadow from his dreamless slumber. There was a chorus of jumbled voices before the door closed once again and light footsteps could be heard coming down the corridor. Shadow remained on the floor; eyes fixed on the ceiling. He tried to figure out how long he had been laying there. It might have been days, maybe weeks. He wasn't even sure if the light he occasionally saw was true sunlight.

He let out a rough cough, "Come to gloat?"

"That would be unbecoming," the Queen stated from the other side of the cell door, "I'll admit my curiosity regarding your condition."

Shadow lifted his featherless wing, "They're still gone."

"And your leg?" the Queen asked.

Shadow slowly rose to his feet, pain coursing through his injured leg, "Spare me your pity."

"Would you prefer I show you mercy?"

"I'd prefer you were dead," Shadow spat. "You may have your people fooled but Iris and I knew the truth."

"And what truth is that?"

"You know very well what truth I speak of," Shadow responded, "Does your King know how you got your crown? Framing your sister for murder?" Shadow suddenly felt himself pulled towards the door.

"Did she tell you how they died?" the Queen asked angrily, a dangerous fire in her eyes. A terrifyingly elegant hand wrapped itself around his neck, "Did she tell you how it was her magic?" Shadow was lifted off his feet, the hand tightening, choking his breath. "How they were found? Burnt black from fire? A fire that had been started by her lighting? I was there. I saw the bolt." As Shadow's vision began to black out the Queen suddenly dropped him to the ground. He landed on his bad leg. It shattered into dust sending a plume of metallic particles into the air. He lay on the floor gasping for breath, the dust filling his lungs as his eyes watered. He coughed harder. He could already feel his son's magic turning his lungs to silver, just as it had his feathers and leg.

"You—" Shadow gasped.

Mirage

"Your life matters not to me *Captain Shadow* and I will take all measures necessary to ensure the safety of my Kingdom and family."

"Like...Like banishing Delmar?" Shadow choked out.

The Queen did not respond. She simply turned and began to walk down the corridor, "Enjoy your last days *Shadow*, the son you attempted to murder has seen to your death."

43. City of the Clouds

Nathan looked out over the crowd of people, all packed tightly around the streets of the city. It reminded him of the race tracks he flew in with the *FireFly*.

"This is crazy," he commented in awe.

Rosa let out a small laugh, "The Guard Race is the biggest event of the year. Everyone turns out to see it."

"Especially after you crashed the first one," Nafais joked from behind on the balcony.

Nathan rolled his eyes, "I believe *daughter* that the only I reason I crashed was because of you."

"Till you ran out of fuel," Nafais responded. Nathan smiled; He was rather enjoying the relationship he was building with Nafais.

"Is Armine running?" Nathan asked.

"Yes, he is," Nafais responded.

"I trust that you gave him a symbol of your affection?" Rosa asked.

Nafais blushed, her wings rustling, "I have not."

"I do believe it would mean a great deal to him," Rosa insisted.

Nafais looked wide-eyed at her mother, her wings raised off her back, as if ready to take flight. "Does this mean..."

"You have never not had my blessing daughter," Rosa answered.

If Nafais could have smiled any bigger it would have split her head in half as she took off towards the racers. Nathan chuckled at his daughter's enthusiasm.

"I am going to have so much fun with Armine," he mused out loud.

"As will I," Rosa answered, her characteristic laugh ringing through the air.

"So, what is she going to give him?" Nathan asked.

"A feather," Rosa answered.

"That's it?"

Rosa nodded, "One of her own feathers, plucked from her wing for him to wear. It is a symbol of great affection and in a more primitive sense tells other women that Armine is hers."

"Huh...that's neat I guess," Nathan responded looking to his feathers.

"It is a custom that is older than my mother was."

"Doesn't that hurt?" Nathan asked, his wings tucked tight against his back.

"Yes, but that is part of the tradition. The willingness to bear the pain in order to show the importance of the other to yourself." Rosa explained. Nathan nodded. "I still wear yours every day."

The Queen pulled out a necklace she had tucked under her gown producing a rough piece of string with a pure white feather attached to it.

"Rosa..." Memories of the day Nathan, or rather Delmar, had given her that feather came flooding into his mind. He couldn't believe she still wore it.

"Traditionally it is only the woman that would give the feather to their love but you were insistent. I always loved how peculiar you could be," Rosa explained. "I still remember my advisor's reactions the first day I wore it. They believed I had taken another lover."

Nathan laughed a little before he stopped, "Had you?"

Rosa let out a short laugh, "No my King. You are my only."

It was then that a horn sounded and the guards took to the air. They rushed through the first turn, Armine in the lead by at least half a wing length. Nathan caught a glimpse of a multi-colored feather tucked into his belt. He looked over the crowd, it seemed every soul in the city was present, eagerly watching the race and cheering on their favored guard. The *Mirage* crew patrolled the sky and streets. Armine had insisted that the city not be left undefended for any reason from this point forward. None of the silver sailors complained as none seemed to have an interest in racing themselves.

A wing pulled him closer to the Queen and he smiled leaning over and kissing her on the cheek as they settled down to watch the race. He was looking forward to seeing Armine take first place. He soon was engrossed in the race. Both himself, and to his delight Rosa, were on the edge of their seats as Armine struggled to maintain his lead. So engrossed were they that Nathan almost

didn't notice the momentary glint of golden wings in the crowd.

Acknowledgments

I would like to acknowledge the contributions of Sharyn Heagle who provided moral and technical support along with knowledge to which I would not otherwise have had access. Without her, this book would not have been possible. Thank you to my mother Betty Gloutney, to Melody Tomka and to Elizabeth Peltz for their assistance in editing this manuscript. Finally, thanks to my family and friends who stood behind me and put up with the process of my writing this manuscript. Thanks to you all.

Patrick Gloutney

Born in Amherst Nova Scotia, Patrick Gloutney moved to Ottawa in 2012 where he pursued his education and career in Aviation. As an active member of the local flying community, he has been the recipient of awards ranging from community involvement to safety and professionalism including the Rockcliffe Flying Club's Ken Chatfield Memorial Trophy for his dedication, enthusiasm, camaraderie, and professionalism in the local flying community. When is not working as a pilot and contributing to the development of his flying community Patrick continues to explore many different avenues in his writing career producing a wide variety of written work.